THE RANSOM ENIGMA

Breakfield and Burkey

Published by

ICABOD Press

ISBN: 978-1-946858-80-1 (paperback)
ISBN: 978-1-946858-79-5 (e-book)

Library of Congress Control Number: 2024912245
Interior and eBook design: F + P Graphic Design, FPGD.com

First Edition
Printed in the United States

MYSTERY | CRIME | SUSPENSE

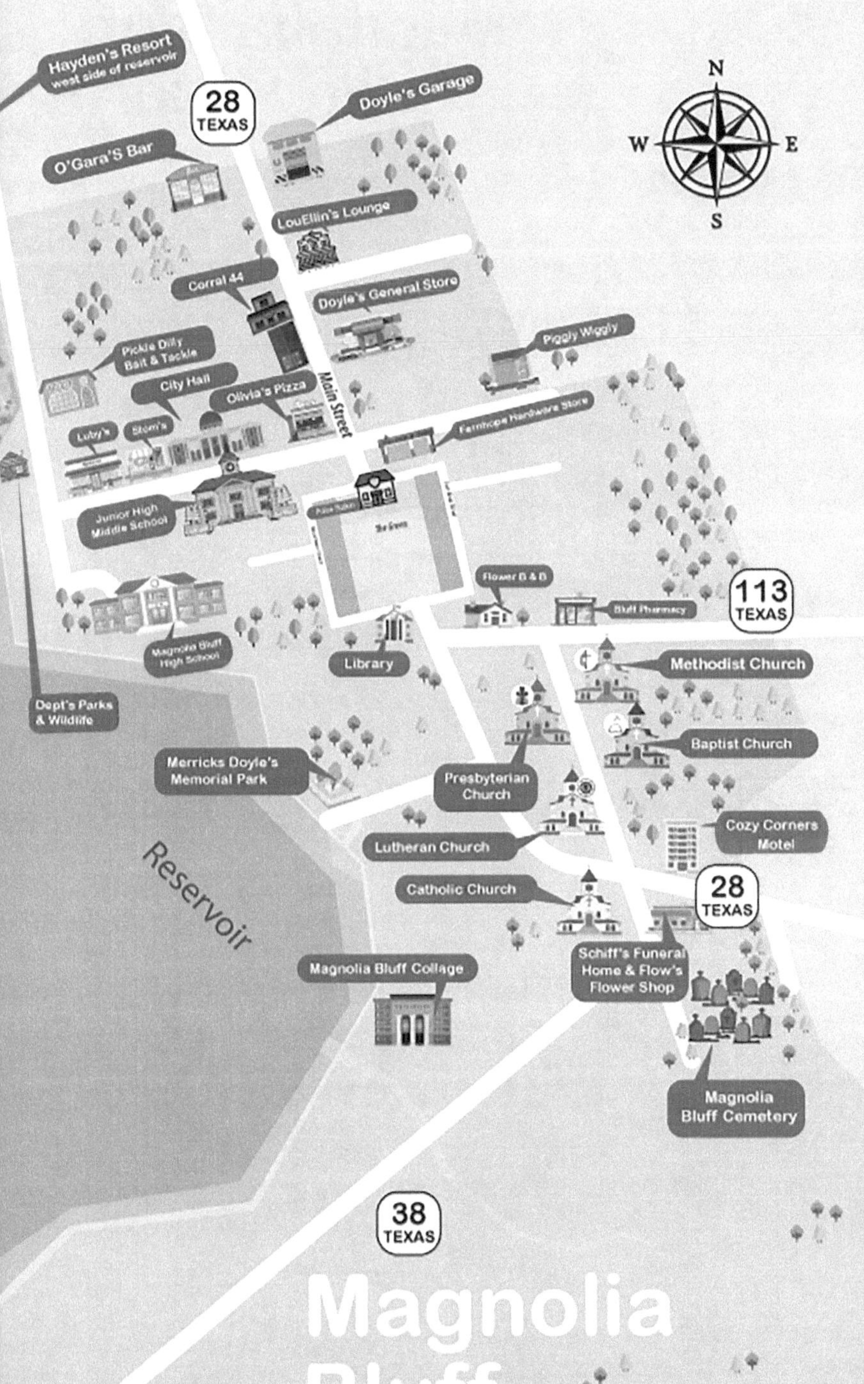

Hayden's Resort
west side of reservoir
O'Gara'S Bar
28 TEXAS
Doyle's Garage
LouEllin's Lounge
Corral 44
Doyle's General Store
Piggly Wiggly
Pickle Dilly Bait & Tackle
City Hall
Olivia's Pizza
Main Street
Farnhope Hardware Store
Luby's
Stom's
Junior High Middle School
Nice Salon
The Green
Flower B & B
Bluff Pharmacy
113 TEXAS
Magnolia Bluff High School
Library
Methodist Church
Dept's Parks & Wildlife
Baptist Church
Merricks Doyle's Memorial Park
Presbyterian Church
Cozy Corners Motel
Reservoir
Lutheran Church
Catholic Church
28 TEXAS
Schiff's Funeral Home & Flow's Flower Shop
Magnolia Bluff Collage
Magnolia Bluff Cemetery
38 TEXAS
Magnolia Bluff
N
W   E
S

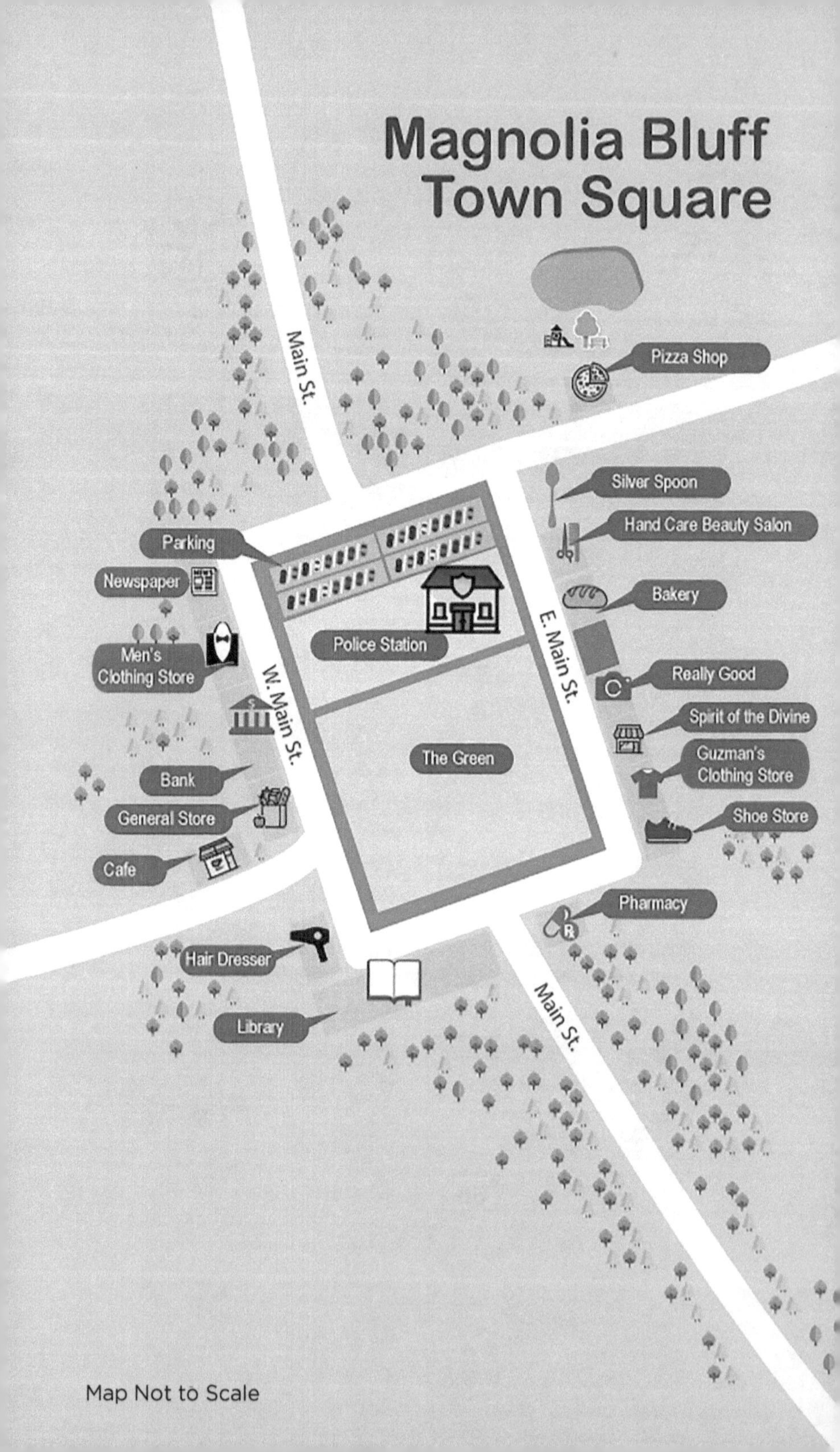

Magnolia Bluff
Town Square

Pizza Shop

Silver Spoon

Hand Care Beauty Salon

Bakery

Really Good

Spirit of the Divine

Guzman's Clothing Store

Shoe Store

Pharmacy

Parking

Newspaper

Men's Clothing Store

Bank

General Store

Cafe

Police Station

The Green

Hair Dresser

Library

Main St.

W. Main St.

E. Main St.

Main St.

Map Not to Scale

It's Almost Perfect

LATE-JULY

JJ Rodreguiz pulled to the locked gate and set the gear to park. He finger-combed his dark, longish hair from his face and beamed. "All right, sweetheart, it is time to wear the blindfold."

"Darn, I was hoping you'd forget," Jo said. "Last time I was here, it was almost finished."

"You're right. I did the final walkthrough a month ago and had them make two changes I know you'll love."

He noticed his wife's kissable pout from the corner of his eye and heard her groan. He rested his hand on her knee. "These are small but perfect modifications, I promise. This house is a big step for us. Indulge me by letting me make it special with a surprise, a carry over the threshold, and a sip of champagne before we start unpacking boxes too numerous to count."

Flashing him a sweet smile, she nodded, her chocolate brown eyes sparkling excitedly, and turned to let him apply the blindfold.

"Thank you, darling." He unlocked the padlock and swung open the gate using his customized mobile application. After he drove through, the sensor box symbol swipe closed the gate automatically. There was no need to re-engage the padlock when they were in residence. The perimeter cameras would capture anyone who entered and provide an alert.

He drove the rental car up to the parking area by the barn, got out, and hurried around the front of the vehicle. He opened her door and helped her out, admiring her shapely, brown legs with his heart racing a few beats. She fit perfectly against his six-foot-two frame. He gently placed her hand in his for the short walk along the vibrant stone path.

She inhaled, "It's so cool to smell the fragrant scent of sage. Are both the white and purple flowering?"

"Yes, they are, plus you'll love the splashes of the emerging shades of pink here and there. These plants will grow and thrive within a few more weeks."

"Can I see?"

"Yes, but later. The line sprinklers running at night optimize water absorption in the summer. There are only a few places where we'll need to hand water. We can stroll along the walkway later, with music drifting from the pergola's speakers." He anticipated her delight at the redesigned parking, which allowed great front and back yard views. "We're almost to the steps."

Jo's pace quickened with her excitement until she almost danced. He swept her into his arms and up the steps. Deftly inserting the key, he opened the door, and his fingers entered the security code. "Honey, our summer home."

She removed her eye covering. Her entire face reflected delight. "Oh, JJ, it's beautiful. The textured walls are rustically elegant." She elbowed him and exclaimed. "That purple accent wall is one of your changes. The pictures we marked for the entrance will pop against that background. Perfect." She hugged and kissed him, then danced from the entry straight ahead to the hallway as he followed, enjoying her enthusiasm. Left went to the bedrooms, with the master at the end. Adjacent to their bedroom was the workout area and two bathrooms.

Jo boisterously laughed. "You're right, honey; there are a lot of boxes."

She raised a hand to her chin and shook her head a bit, which made her long hair swing in shiny dark waves that reminded him of Expresso.

"Boy, I'm glad I tagged the rooms on some of them. It'll make it faster to unpack." She hugged him. "Thank you for the extra effort. It's lovely. The blinds we picked when open brighten the space. They will make it easier to focus on paintings and nicknacks."

JJ laughed. "I know how you love your nicknacks. I had Jason open the windows and doors for several days to help it air out."

"I don't smell paint or varnish at all. I smell a bit of potpourri in each room: light, fresh scents. These accentuate the bright colors of the accent-colored walls."

"We can easily repaint any of them if your artist's eye moves you. I tried to match the fragrances from our Brazil home that I know you love."

She wrapped her arm around his waist and hugged him. "Perfect."

"Let's peek into the kitchen, formal dining room, living room, library, my office, and the garden room, which also exits to the pergola. I believe you'll be pleased."

They retraced their steps down the hallway to explore the other rooms. Boxes were stacked everywhere. Jo tugged his hand toward the garden room, where he'd set up the furniture so they could enjoy it immediately. "You chose well, husband."

"It seemed like the perfect place to start the day with access to the fresh air." Pressing a button on the wall panel opened the rectangle-carved wooden boxes scattered over the dance floor. Large chrome and crystal pendant lights lowered, sending light streams across the entire pergola. "I think these are reminiscent of a Cabaret," he said. The slight press of another button allowed slow jazz music to fill the area. Holding out his hand, he said, "Dance with me."

They expertly executed a Slow Balboa across the golden oak-like vinyl dance floor. Even with tables and chairs, ample dance space was available. As the song ended, JJ pulled her into his arms and kissed her. They looked up as two cars and a four-wheeler approached.

Jo raised an eyebrow. "What's this, company with a hundred boxes? Oh, JJ."

Chagrined by the impromptu friends' arrival when his thoughts had drifted toward more than dancing, he added another squeeze. "Yep, and our work crew to help us unpack. They volunteered to do this before we arrived, but I insisted you be the placement director for the contents. Ann agreed but still wanted to help." He frowned. "I believe I lost track of time." He tapped her gently on the tip of her nose. "We'll get back to dancing later."

Jo rubbed her hands together, laughing. "Okay, open some champagne, please. Let's toast and git er done."

JJ chuckled. "Sweetheart, let Lily do the twang; your Brazilian accent made that sound odd."

She playfully punched his shoulder as the crowd of friends rushed into the pergola with hugs and congrats on them finally arriving.

Lily raced toward them like a twenty-year-old rather than a fifty-something, her dark hair bouncing around her oval face and intense light blue eyes. She hugged them both. "Ann, Hank, Camila, Renata, and I are here, ready to attack the bedrooms. JJ said the beds and main dressers are positioned exactly as you diagrammed them." She patted Jo's back. "Very smart, my dear, I might add. We can unpack the boxes, and you can indicate where stuff goes. Jason is ready to set nails and picture hooks where you indicate. Renata will take notes to ensure Jo's directions are followed."

Renata held up her notepad in her slender brown fingers.

Jason's mother, Joyce, smiled and offered, "I'll pitch in wherever."

Jo smiled. "That sounds perfect. We have four bedrooms to set up, so helpers pick your targets. I thought I'd unbox the kitchen first, followed by the dining room, the living room, and the garden room. JJ, you'll want to do your office and the work-out room."

JJ saluted. "Yes, ma'am. Jason and I can set up the exercise equipment while everyone unboxes in your assigned rooms. We'll come to help hang stuff when we finish." He clapped the teen on the back. "Of course, you can use the gear whenever you want."

"Thanks, JJ. At least I'll know the purpose of each item. Will you teach me some of the martial arts stuff later on?"

"Sure. We are here for two months on holiday. Ann, Jo will speak with you and Lily about her idea for our neighborhood party," JJ clarified.

Hank stuck out his rugged hand. "Glad we're finally neighbors. Ann's been talking for weeks about how much she wants to help Jo. We wouldn't have our girls if it weren't for you and your pretty wife. Pour the bubbly, then let's get to work. Time is ticking."

"You helped get us this property, so I think we're even," JJ said, clapping his rancher friend on the back.

Several hours later, the four women relaxed at a table set up in the pergola. The kids and men took the boxes and packing materials to the temporary trash container by the entry gate. Jo carried a new bottle of open champagne and refilled all the glasses with a smile.

"Thank you," Jo said.

Lily commented, "That unpacking worked out better than I thought. Of course, your organization made it easier, sweetie."

Jo inclined her head with a sly smile. "I try."

Joyce said, "JJ indicated you wanted a housewarming party. What's your vision for that?"

"We are so attached to this community." Jo waved her arms to indicate everyone. "You've made JJ and me feel so welcome. The idea of having a party with music, food, a little drinking, and dancing out here is like a give-back."

Ann asked, "Who do you want to invite?"

"Everyone in Magnolia Bluff. This town has some delightfully unique and crazy loveable characters," Jo said.

"Characters," repeated Lily. "Now you're talking about Mary Lou, I bet."

They all chuckled, and Jo blushed.

Lily thrummed her fingers on the metal tabletop, sounding like a muted kettledrum. "Renata and I can make the sides and hors d'oeuvres: fruit salads, green salads, sausage balls, mini quesadillas, stuffed mushrooms, and desserts…like brownies."

"I can do some fruit punches, cupcakes, and cookies," Ann added.

"I would love to do the invites," said Joyce. "It'll allow me to send notes to everyone in town. If you don't mind a plug for my real-estate role, I'll do some advertising to help with rental property, summer homes, second homes, and ranchland. Yesterday, I rented three homes with one-year leases and spoke to a gentleman today about another rental. He's going to confirm tomorrow. My commissions this month are outstanding." She took another swallow of champagne. "Thankfully, I'll get that money just in time to take Jason shopping for school clothes. I swear he grows like a weed these days."

"Joyce," Jo petitioned, "please have everyone reply to us at our family email address, which you already have. Afterward, I can send everyone a thank you and well wishes." She reached over and patted Joyce's hand, admiring her porcelain skin. "You're raising a fine young man, Joyce. We appreciate you letting him help with the property when we're out of town." Sipping her bubbles, she looked at her friends. "After all this work today, you don't mind helping with a party in a few weeks? I love all your ideas. We'll barbecue the meats out here, provide all types of beverages, and get to meet everyone."

Lily raised her glass. "Here's to the best party housewarming Magnolia Bluff has ever seen."

"Cheers!" they all chorused.

CHAPTER 1

It's Going to Be a Great Day

By Texas Hill Country standards, the day began with a surprising chill to the air. The early morning sprinklers at Lily's Bed & Breakfast doused the flowers and lawn with a gentle mist, enough to keep the blooms and foliage invitingly bright for another August day. Summer in Magnolia Bluff remained relatively mild, yet the sun was ready to kiss the hundred-degree mark at any moment.

Lily began at sunrise with determination and a spring in her step, intermixed with off-key singing to country songs as she checked off the assigned tasks. Her hours of whirlwind activities included gathering fresh blossoms and greenery for the dining room table vases and supervising Renata's food prep for the regular breakfast customers who trickled in at nine. Yanking out the soft, thick hair tie, she shook her black hair that brushed her shoulders and grinned at the image of the incoming caller.

"Jo, honey, good morning. Before you ask, we're making great progress. I have cut flowers in buckets outside and ready for pick up. Don't worry; my army and I are crossing things off your checklist left and right." She laughed. "Yep, Renata and I are like a small army with what we've accomplished so far. She's a treasure in the kitchen. I got her a new apron that reads *Mad Chopper*, for her live-action mode. My biggest challenge is keeping her knives sharp. Everything is coming together without any hitches."

Chuckling, Jo admitted, "Actually, Lily, I was calling to see if I could help. I can grab the buckets later or send JJ if you want my help with the food preparation. I've been counting the number of guests who accepted the invite, and I'm afraid you and Renata will work so hard you won't enjoy yourselves at the party tonight. JJ's handling the meat grilling here on his new barbecue with several secret sauces, so I'm available to help."

Lily cackled, "Hon, don't worry about a thing. We have enough sides and desserts to feed the county. We might want to get some containers so folks can take the leftovers home. If we run short, I'll put another scoop of lard into the dishes to make them go farther."

Jo laughed. "Oh, Lily, the imagery you painted in my mind reminds me there are some things one can't unhear."

Lily chuckled with a snort. She recalled Jo's pretty face with her big, expressive, expresso-black eyes underlined by her beautiful smile, like the spread in the fashion magazine that arrived last week. "Made you look."

"I should know how much you tease by now, but you still catch me and bring me up short. I am glad you have extra flowers; mine are trying, but I don't have enough for the few vases I wanted inside. Thanks. I'll head your way. The offer stands if you need an extra set of hands."

"I don't have anything at this point that requires your cast iron skillet expertise," Lily chortled.

Jo laughed, and Lily disconnected. Then, she slid the phone into her apron pocket and tapped her hands to the familiar Willy song playing in the kitchen. She checked another item off the list and contentedly sighed as she began setting the breakfast tables. Her heartfelt singing stopped when she heard the front door chime, suggesting someone had entered. She cocked her head to listen.

A deep, husky voice hollered from the foyer, "Lily, it's Graham. Do you have a minute?"

She wrinkled her nose, wondering what was up and if he was socializing or asking for current gossip. "Huston, I'm in the kitchen headed into the dining room. I don't mind jawing, but I'm not yelling across the house, even if I don't have any over-nighters."

The consummate newspaperman, hoping for a cup of her coffee, said, "Oh good. I was afraid I'd catch you in a bad mood or too busy helping with the catering for Jo and JJ's party. On my way, sweetie."

Lily picked up the coffee pot and an extra mug for the buffet table and looked at Renata. "Hon, when you start thinking about the kind of guy you want in your life, try to avoid grumpy ones who think they know everything." She turned to leave out the swinging door, then stopped and looked over her shoulder. "That's a pretty tall assignment now that I think about it."

The slender five-foot-four Hispanic sixteen-year-old grinned and flipped her head so fast that her dark-brown braided ponytail spun around and landed on her shoulder. She picked up the chef knife and aimed it toward her temple. "I'll let you know when I'm older."

The swinging door was open, and Graham leaned against the jamb with a sour expression. "Ol' Lily, you never change," he said. "You never admit to being bossy, but you know what everyone should be doing."

Lily frowned, indignant at the directed judgment. "Huston, you came to my place. I don't like your attitude, especially when you want a cup of this coffee," she added, raising the pot. She looked at her treasured helper, who bit back a smile and returned to her cutting. Then, she pushed past the source of her annoyance into the dining room to continue checking off the chore list.

"What's on your mind?" Lily placed the coffee mugs on the buffet and filled one for him. Annoyed, she resumed setting the tables, not bothering to face him.

"My social sources tell me you're whipping up half the town to join the Rodreguiz housewarming party. Most businesses are closing early. Rumor has it the plans include food and an open bar. They seem like mighty generous folks to foot the bill for everyone to come and enjoy themselves."

"You got that right. They are. A DJ is being brought in from LouEllen's club to spin some music for dancing, should anyone feel inclined to go boot-scooting."

From the corner of her eye, Lily noticed Graham rub his jaw as he sipped the mug of coffee, forming the words in his mind before speaking.

"From my viewpoint, our town should be throwing the party for them after everything they've done for this community. Two years ago, they helped derail the human trafficking scum, and last year, they resolved the Thomas and Marissa Stevens mystery."

Lily guffawed. "Why, Huston, I had no idea you cared. You could always bring some of your favorite adult beverages as a gesture. The event is a housewarming for them."

"I like 'em, but not that much."

Lily roared with laughter. "Everyone will be there. Why not put your sorry backside in the middle of the festivities this afternoon so you can do a fine job reporting the event."

Before Graham could argue further about her advice, Lily's phone played *Pick Me Up* by Gabby Barrett. She answered and began talking at two hundred words a minute with gusts double that and beyond.

Graham moved into her line of sight. She wiggled a few fingers goodbye and watched as he covered his ears.

Jo waited to hand him the needed items as she watched JJ wire another video camera along the driveway. She appreciated his broad shoulders and lean, muscular build. He kept fit with routine martial arts practice and helped her maintain a trim figure for her modeling. The exercise room was the ideal place to twist out the kinks after holding different poses for what felt like hours and stay fit.

He commented, "Honey, when the gate is open, I like knowing when folks are coming to visit us. It's a bonus if we identify them before they knock on the door." His grin made her heart thump faster, especially as he brushed his black hair behind his ear. "That way," he added, nudging her shoulder and lowering his voice, "if it's someone we don't want to talk to, we can sneak out the back and then run like crazy to Hank and Ann's."

Jo giggled. "Like the salesman who came by last week. I felt so sad for him and his challenging stammer. He tried hard to talk us into buying a bible for our new home."

JJ shook his head. "Me too. I stopped feeling too sorry when he promised to come by daily and read us some passages if we didn't want to buy one. Best con job I've ever seen."

"It was nice of you to buy the whole box. Now, we have gifts for guests who laugh when you tell the story tonight. We've accomplished a lot since we moved in a couple of weeks ago."

JJ finished wiring up the last camera he'd mounted on a stick, masquerading as a flower. He climbed from the ladder and brushed his hands together. "Yes, we have. The cameras are finally distributed. I'll test all the connections. When I verify that they are each recording and communicating with the host system, I'll put two cameras in the front room. That way—"

Jo interrupted, "JJ, can we please just let it go with placing them along the driveway or outside? I don't want our house armed with intrusive cameras capturing pictures of people maybe straightening their clothes or probing for unwanted ear wax."

He sulked like a little boy who wanted all the toys. She chuckled.

"I'm sorry, babe. I'm probably over-rotating on the security. I shouldn't be suspicious of our Magnolia Bluff neighbors. Everyone's been so helpful. Remarkably, they don't pry into what we do when we aren't here. We're safe and sound in our home, away from the limelight like you wanted."

Jo pulled him into a hug. "JJ, I'm glad you're thinking about our privacy. I feel comfortable here. I don't want our private moments captured on video. However, I want to understand how your program works and how to save files if needed when you're busy or away."

In a mischievous mood, JJ waggled his eyebrows. "You're sure you don't want one in the master bedroom?"

She punched his shoulder and growled. "I'm certain that's not happening."

JJ shot her an evil smirk, dogging the subject. "I promise I won't post those videos, like the others, looking for votes on the internet."

Jo rattled, and her stomach churning flared.

JJ laughed. "Made you look. You're so much fun to tease."

She pursed her lips.

"All right, the subject's been sent to Pluto, where there is no internet, so no more nonsense."

Jo let go of the breath she hadn't realized she held. "You can be so exasperating sometimes. I'm in front of the camera modeling when I work. I don't want them in our home. I appreciate being secure, so thank you. But I want this house separate from our professional lives. No one here knows who I am except Chief Tommy and Lily. When we're in Magnolia Bluff, we can live normal lives. I don't want to think about the social parasites that have ruined so much at home in Brazil. Here we're free."

JJ pulled her into a tight embrace and stroked her back, increasing her sense of reassurance. He whispered in her ear. "We're safe, secure, and together."

CHAPTER 2

You're All Invited

J oyce drove to the house shortly after lunch, with Camila and Jason following on horseback. They volunteered to help Jo and JJ prepare for the evening.

Jo waved as she got out of the truck. "Your timing is perfect, kids. I picked up four buckets of flowers and could use your help creating the arrangements for the patio."

Camila dismounted and tied her mare to the hitching post by the barn, instructing Jason to do likewise. Jo grinned, knowing the teen's long, brownish-black hair and dark complexion always got second looks from folks seeing her for the first time. Jason was strong and athletic but a little reticent in most social surroundings. His dark tan and sun-streaked brown hair suggested hours of outdoor activities. JJ had confided to Jo that Camila and horseback riding had given that young man extra confidence.

Joyce rolled down the window as Jo approached. "I'm showing a couple of houses today and won't be able to help. If all y'all are falling behind, please holler. I'll call Brandon to see if he can join early. He plans to bring Max. Max can hoover up stray crumbs, but Brandon is the crumb dispenser, so you gotta watch him." She grinned.

Jo sensed JJ behind her, and she confirmed this when he looped his arm over her shoulder and kissed her cheek. "Hey, Joyce," said JJ. "Is Brandon any good at bartending? Tommy promised he'd be here for that chore, but he might be late if he gets a call. We have more people who accepted our invites than I expected. Without bartending help, I'll burn the steaks and burgers."

Joyce nodded. "I'm not sure. He likes opening beers and offering to others, but I've never seen him mix a drink. He's not Chief Tommy, who's more inclined to tell someone they've been overserved and cut them off."

They all chuckled.

"Nothing like a police chief bartender to help keep people sober enough to drive home and not get ticketed," said JJ.

"I'm sure we'll be good," Jo added. "We wanted to thank you with a modest toast for helping us prepare this place for tonight. Max is more than welcome to perform the crumb-hunting chore."

JJ inclined his head toward the teens. "Camila, Hank, and Ann are planning to come, aren't they? I'm a little surprised Ann isn't already here supervising."

Camila chuckled. "Dad fixed it so he and Momma could arrive shortly before the start so you wouldn't have anyone helping things to death. Lily called several times to coordinate their arrival in time to unload all the food she and Renata were preparing. Renata just got her license and is excited to drive one of the food trucks. Jo, I can help you with the flowers."

"Great. Joyce, we'll see you later," said Jo with a slight wave. She turned and headed toward her truck with Camila. They reached into the pickup bed to move the buckets to the ground for carrying. She was grateful they would each have two containers for balance as they brought them to the expansive patio.

"Honey, Jason and I will start setting up the extra tables and chairs," JJ suggested.

"Perfect. The tablecloths are stacked by the bar."

JJ watched the various camera feeds in the different segments on the multiple monitors. He turned up the sound as Lily and her caravan showed up mid-afternoon. Lily pulled to the first spot, then leaped out to direct the three other trucks. He admired her agility and take-charge attitude as she arranged the vehicles for ease of departure and not to clog the guest traffic. Renata, who was in the last truck, did well until she tried to back up. Lily must have sensed the danger to the other vehicles, the fence, and the trees.

She hollered with a smile and a nod to the teen. "All right, sweetheart, I'll take it from here. Put the truck in park, please. Your vehicle is key, so let me position it exactly where we need it. Like putting a puzzle together, it takes experience."

Pouting, the girl shoved the vehicle into park and stepped out with a frown and tears threatening.

Lily rushed up and hugged her with a big smile. "You have the desserts, so we need to get them unloaded and put them into the coolers at the far end of the dance floor. You did fantastic. I'm very proud of you."

JJ was pleased with the synchronization of the audio video feeds to the four large touchscreen monitors and surround sound transmission inside his state-of-the-art geek office, called, "Honey, the catering team is here. Can you go and soothe Renata's ego? Thankfully, Lily saw the danger and intercepted a problem before our front yard became a bumper car extravaganza."

Jo hurried outdoors with the video feed capturing her sincere smile. He knew her soft demeanor would effectively smooth ruffled feathers. He watched the crew as they busied themselves, unloading the food, shuttling it to the designated areas, either inside the kitchen, at the breakfast bar, the cooler by the grilling area, or the built-in refrigerators at the far side.

JJ was concerned when he heard Jo remark, "Lily, you've over-amped on quantities. No matter how terrific it looks and smells, we'll never get through this much food. I hope you brought those to-go containers because I'm not sure we have enough space for what I expect we'll have left."

He watched, feeling relieved as Lily smirked and gently patted Jo's cheek.

"You're so young, Jo. Get used to feeding Texans like I have. We'll be lucky to get through the evening without running to the store for something to hold them over."

Jo's bewildered expression made Lily chuckle harder.

About that time, another delivery truck appeared. The driver got out and yelled, "Delivery for JJ Rodreguiz."

JJ rushed outside and approached the man. "Yes!" He raised his fist toward the sky. "Perfect timing, sir, with the alcohol and soft drinks to wash down the food. Please bring the delivery to the outdoor patio to the left, where I'm setting up the bar. Did you happen to bring extra ice?"

The driver looked at the distance, twitching his mouth as if considering the safest route. He clucked his tongue and suggested, "Yeah, I have extra ice. Let me get my dolly. If you'll help guide me, we can take it in two trips, maybe three."

JJ, sensing tension, offered, "I've got a hand truck. Let me get it, and you can follow me."

The man visibly brightened. "Thanks, man."

JJ chuckled and noticed Jo watching with her lip caught under her teeth. Trying to read her mind, he said, "By the way, you'll still get a good tip."

A short time later, but still in mid-chaos, the happy liquor delivery man drove off, and Ann marched in with Hank in tow.

"All right," Ann said. "Let's get this organized, people. If I leave it up to you, we'll still be setting up this time tomorrow."

Camila went to her dad's side, hugged him, and whispered in his ear. "I thought you would stall her a little longer."

"See how well it worked?" he guffawed. "We could've been here hours ago if I hadn't helped her in the kitchen. I paid for the delay." He rubbed his knuckles. "She whacked me with her giant soup spoon and told me to stop helping. I did the best I could."

Camila added a sympathetic nod and hugged him again. "I understand."

The rest of the afternoon was a cacophony of barked orders, people bumping into one another or the tables, and food containers organized and reorganized until Lily and Ann were satisfied.

JJ distributed the adult beverages early to get the combatants mellowed out in time for the guests.

Jo scooted next to his side and hip-bumped him. "We're gonna have fun."

CHAPTER 3

It's Fun Until Someone Cries Foul

The music was soft and relaxing inside the house, but the pergola and dance floor area delivered had high-volume, non-stop requested songs heavy on country/western music. True to her word, LouEllen brought her best DJ, Stan, from the bar. He captured the party's mood and projected a sense of fun to the guests. Stan applauded great dance moves and solicited favorites for his playlist.

Jo liked Stan's attitude and the way he took advantage of every opportunity to keep the excitement going. It was pleasantly warm but not oppressive for the dancers. She placed a cold beer by him, receiving a grin and nod of appreciation. Jo spotted LouEllen doing a two-step toward the grill to place her steak order. Jo recalled Lily's warning to keep LouEllen from getting too close to JJ. She edged close to the near side by JJ as LouEllen sauntered over, licking her lips as her eyes completed the head-to-toe inventory of her husband.

"Jo, I placed my order for medium steak. Hank's cooking it." She batted her made-up eyes. "Just one little two-step on the dance floor with your drop-dead-gorgeous man, please."

Jo relented with a laugh. "One two-step, LouEllen, but keep your hands off."

JJ grinned at Jo when she kissed his cheek. He eye-rolled when LouEllen grabbed his arm and navigated them to an open spot. Jo heard a *maybe* followed by laughter from the woman as the song began. LouEllen wasn't a bad-looking woman, a bit heavy by fifty kilograms and twice JJ's age. She knew if that were the price for their DJ, he'd brave it.

Jo laughed as JJ tried to keep step with LouEllen as she kicked up her heels and lifted her skirt in between blatant backside grabbing. Several guests gave them room and clapped as JJ twirled his dance partner to dodge her hands.

JJ moved next to Jo, who had her back against the stone half-wall and counter extension from the grill. He draped his arm over her shoulder, giving her a quick kiss. "Honey, please don't offer me as an item in the produce section to her again. I'm like bruised fruit by now."

Jo smirked. "Was it good for you?" She pressed a folded bill into his shirt pocket. "Here's your cut of the extra bribe LouEllen paid, and Stan can stay until the party ends. The crowd loves his playlist."

JJ laughed. "As long as it's only one dance, we can donate that to charity. Stan's great. Let me know when you're ready to Tango. I checked, and he has one."

Joyce, Brandon, and Max arrived as the afternoon sun approached the horizon. Jo walked up to them. "Welcome. I'm glad you made it. The salads are inside, with your son helping to serve them. Beverages are by the bar near the grill, with Hank and JJ working those areas."

"The food looks and smells amazing. I didn't think I was hungry until I saw the steak and potato salad," Brandon said. "I can help with the bar if the crowd grows. May I let Max roam? He won't hurt a soul, doesn't jump on folks or tables, but he will keep the floor clean."

Jo chuckled as she patted the sleek black coat of the retriever. "That's fine with me. I've heard he's a good boy. We wanted to wait until sunset, when most folks are here, to toast you, Joyce, and Jason."

"It's unnecessary." Joyce smoothed her stylish floral print A-line dress. "I would like a glass of wine before eating."

"I'll grab a white for you and a beer for me," Brandon offered. "Jo, would you like anything?"

She shook her head and grinned. According to Joyce, Brandon was in his mid-forties. He'd retired from the New York police department after a distinguished career as a narcotics detective. He'd rarely left the East Coast until he moved to Magnolia Bluff last year. Jo suspected he was still in culture shock, though he likely wouldn't admit it. The pair looked cute together. It was clear Joyce was smitten as her bright eyes followed his movements to the bar.

"Joyce, is he a keeper?" Jo asked.

She sighed, "Oh, my, yes. He's never been married except to his work and has no children, though he and Jason seem to have bonded. The poor man has no siblings, and his parents passed away." Her eyes twinkled as she grinned mischievously. "I like him more than a lot."

Jo patted Joyce's arm. "Then, I'm certain he's a keeper for you, girl."

Brandon returned with their drinks, and they clinked glasses.

"Feel free to dance. I need to get Max a bowl of water, then mingle," said Jo.

Joyce guided Brandon, introducing him to a few people. They picked at some food Camila had on a tray as she worked her way through the crowd, offering samples.

Jo walked inside, finding a few folks mingling in small groups. She looked around and noticed happy people chatting. She grabbed a bowl for Max. "Jason, your mom is on the patio. Do you and Camila feel stuck in here?" She said in a relaxed, confident tone, "You seem to have things running like a fine Swiss watch."

Jason grinned. "We're good. Camila decided we were going to be waiters. Renata is assembling trays for us to take around." He popped a sausage ball into his mouth. "All the food is terrific. If there are any of these left over, I'm happy to carry them home."

She patted his shoulder. "Good to know."

Jo returned outside and filled the bowl with water, placing it outside the dancing area. Max made a beeline for it, so she looked over the crowd while he nearly drained it. She refilled it and set it on the floor, then noticed Tommy had arrived.

She rushed over and gave him a side hug. Chief Tommy Jager was about five inches taller, but his black Stetson made him appear loftier and not quite so menacing. "I'm glad you could make it. Brandon can help tend the bar, too, if you need a break."

"I got this, Jo." Tommy set his jaw and walked toward the bar and grill area. Several guests greeted him; some shared quick hugs.

Behind the bar, next to JJ, he pulled several sheets of paper from the inside pocket of his jacket and spread them on the table. JJ eyed them curiously.

Tommy stated, "I have nearly everyone's name who I knew was coming. Nobody gets over-served then let loose to drive home." JJ acknowledged the request, adding ticks to those he'd already served.

Jo shook her head with a grin. She pulled JJ aside and handed him a glass of wine.

JJ borrowed the mic from Stan. "Everyone, we wanted to toast our friends, Lily, Joyce, Tommy, and Hank's family for making this party a reality. Cheers!"

A unified "Cheers!" roared from the guests.

"And to you," Jo added, "new friends, thank you for making us feel welcome in Magnolia Bluff. Cheers!"

A mix of *Cheers and Glad you're here"* was returned as people returned to eating and drinking.

JJ returned the mic. Jo took his arm, and they mingled. She whispered in his ear, between learning new names and faces, "I'm glad we did this party, honey. I think it's a huge success."

JJ nodded. "The colors of the brilliant red and golden sunset are stunning. It seems to signal time for the older folks to say their goodbyes." He pointed to a few folks making the goodbye circuit.

"I was worried we had too much food. But it disappeared faster than I imagined. Since Tommy arrived, the drink allocation has been stingier, too," she chuckled.

"The dancing is intense. Look at the teens putting extra moves on the country favorites. Are you ready for a Tango, sweetheart?"

She squeezed his arm and said, "Later. I'm enjoying being with you."

JJ and Jo circulated among the guests to keep the conversation flowing. Jo listened to Joyce reminding folks of the current real estate market in the area and how much she could help if they needed a change.

Lily pulled Jo aside. "Hon, we're almost out of food. Hank cooked the remaining meats with two platters on the warmer for folks to grab. If I'd known everyone would show up and eat like a field hand, I'd have doubled the amounts."

Jo grinned. "We have a small amount of alcohol and soft beverages remaining." She squeezed Lily. "It means the house-warming is almost over. No worries. It's time to wind things down."

Tommy must have heard her because he yelled, "Last call!"

Hank and Ann stuck around, though Jo could see Hank was ready to leave. JJ asked Stan for one last song before calling it a night. A few took advantage of the final dance while others went to their vehicles for an orderly departure down the roads; some walked, others in cars.

Most of the young people had disappeared except for Jason, Renata, and Camila. Joyce, Brandon, and Lily added cups and plates to the trash bags. Tommy wiped down the bar and grill area, producing a bottle of the excellent whiskey he'd held back, and collared everyone to gather around. A small quantity of the golden liquid was carefully poured into small shot glasses for one final toast.

"To our new neighbors," he proposed. "May your blessings be generous, and your troubles be slight."

Lily tossed hers back and put her glass out for another. Tommy frowned. She smirked. "What? What? I've not had one, Tommy. Check your list."

Tommy grudgingly obliged, then jammed the cork back into the whiskey bottle, signaling the bar was closed.

Jo noted the time. "Thank you all. Leave the rest of this for us to clear away. You've been wonderful."

Jo and JJ hugged folks, saying farewells and promising to talk soon.

Tommy joined Jo and JJ inside the house. They grabbed used plates and glasses, adding them to Tommy's trash bag.

Jo spotted an envelope under the edge of the flower vase on the coffee table. Easing it free, she saw it was addressed to her. She smiled. "JJ, someone was kind enough to leave a note for us. This reminds me of that time in Brazil when the techno-geeks, Rox and Charles, came for B-B-Q Brazilian style at our home. They left some small but thoughtful thank-you gifts. Someone has done the same here."

Jo opened the envelope, slipped out a sheet of white paper, and unfolded it. She read the typed message and gasped. Slumping into the sofa, she burst into tears.

Alarmed, JJ snatched the letter and read it with Tommy looking over his shoulder.

> JoW, the Brazilian super-model, is hiding in Texas.
>
> I know who you are.
>
> If you don't want everyone to find your hiding place,
>
> Pay me $100,000 in cryptocurrency in two days.
>
> It's just chump change for you.
>
> I'll contact you with instructions. **Tell no one.**

JJ stormed, "No one threatens my wife, the blackmailing bastard. I'll kill him."

"Put down the letter, JJ," Tommy said. "Don't touch it or the envelope again. Get a baggie, and I'll have it checked for prints." He reread it. "There are two people in town who know who you are, Jo: me and Lily. When you arrived, someone else stumbled over that or recognized you from a newspaper photo. We'll start looking tomorrow. JJ, you need to stay out of it, please. Let me do my job."

JJ fretted over Jo well into the night. He coaxed her into a bubble bath, followed by a gentle massage with lotion until she fell asleep. JJ, angry at the awful end to their party, decided to research their current problem. He sent an email to his second in command, Brayson, in the Luxembourg CATS headquarters, with a picture of the blackmail note. Fortunately, it was early for Brayson. "On it," returned in seconds.

JJ reviewed the videos filmed during their party for faces that seemed out of place. He then sent Brayson the access link for analysis using their advanced facial recognition programs. Rubbing his face, he mumbled, "I'm too tired to focus. I need a couple of hours of sleep." He groaned with a giant, unstifled yawn. "I wish I had added the living room cameras, even though I agree with Jo that's not how we want to live. But a video of the slimy bastard leaving the letter would have put us ahead."

JJ drifted back to where Jo slept. Her fitful moves and mumbled words reinforced his anxiety about ending this blackmail attack.

Jo shot up in bed and cried, "No, no!"

It took many minutes to calm her. He draped his arm over her for reassurance before drifting off.

CHAPTER 4

Witnesses

JJ awoke early Sunday morning after endless nightmares battling shadowy monsters. He slipped soundlessly from bed. Glancing at her form, he was grateful Jo seemed to be in a deep sleep. The muted outside light was a leftover from the full moon, which would soon give way to sunrise. Tiptoeing from their bedroom, he pressed the light on in his office. He noted everything was connected as the machines hummed to life. He twisted to get the kinks out. "I should go for a quick workout to get the blood flowing," he mumbled. Password entry and secondary authentication were completed, and he waited for the standard programs to load. The screens brightened with the daily news feeds. "Kicking or hitting something has appeal. I'd hate to break my new equipment," he mused.

A large picture of the threatening note appeared on his left screen. It stated *I'll contact you soon*. It failed to define the contact method. Methodically, he picked the note apart, making notes. The envelope was addressed to JoW, not him. Tommy confirmed the small circle of people who realized Jo's identity as JoW, Destiny Fashion supermodel. He wanted to believe no friend of theirs would hurt Jo. They wanted a quiet community where she could relax and make friends. He smacked his hand on the desktop. "I didn't take enough precautions to keep her safe."

Most of the party invitations were emailed by Mr. and Mrs. Rodreguiz. The information provided their house address, notations about parking outside the property, and an RSVP request. The RSVP was a reply to the invite with their names, address, and number of attendees. They pre-printed name tags that folks could pick up inside the house after arrival. The address request was to allow Jo to send a handwritten thank-you note and to start a Christmas card list. Jo, Lily, Ann, Joyce, and he had access to that email account, primarily for planning the food. Lily and Ann knew most of the folks in town. Knowing the guests made it easy to care for known allergies or preferences when they suggested the sides, desserts, and quantities.

A couple of Hank's hands had run the four-wheeler like a shuttle service for those who didn't want to stroll in. The camera video feeds captured those walking or riding. These he'd sent to Brayson last evening.

Launching the email, he found no new messages and, surprisingly, no spam. Pressing the refresh button yielded nothing. "Come on, you miserable weasel, send an email. All I need is a starting point," he argued.

His instant message window pinged. It was from Brayson.

Anything on your side yet?

He typed a response.

Not yet. Let's parse the images from the video feeds.

Brayson replied.

It shouldn't take too long. Why?

JJ typed.

I want to add names and cross-check
the email RSVPs we received.

Brayson's fingers moved according to the moving dots.

Good idea. We can look for outliers and
optimize our facial recognition.

JJ's phone displayed Chief Tommy's face with a text to open the gate. He cocked his head, hoping the man had a lead. He released the gate from his phone app and proceeded to the side door through the garden room to minimize the noise on the bedroom side of the house.

Tommy parked close and got out. "Morning, JJ. I figured you'd be up before the sun. Is Jo up too?"

"No, it was late when she finally slept. I can brew coffee for us if you want. I've been reviewing everything."

"Yes, coffee, but add some water to mine if you're doing the Brazilian style. I can only tolerate so much caffeine before I've eaten." Tommy smiled weakly, then followed JJ inside.

"We had some fruit left and those rolls. Help yourself to anything in the refrigerator." JJ put the coffee on. "I've been scribbling notes trying to make sense of the *how* because I haven't a clue on the *who*." He filled two cups and handed Tommy the one with the extra water. "Come on, I'll show you what I have so far."

Tommy followed JJ into the office, letting out a low whistle as his eyes captured all the visuals. "Three big screens by a workstation. Geeze, JJ, no wonder you can always find stuff."

"The note you're aware of because you have the original."

"Yep, and I have a buddy working to see if we have any prints. I still have yours and Jo's from last year, which I can use for elimination. I really can't believe you've been here for less than three weeks and are already stepping in something," Tommy stated with a slight shake of his head.

"I know. It's not making me happy, especially since Jo is so upset."

JJ reviewed his list with Tommy. "I will assemble isolated shots from the video feeds. I hope you can help match names to faces for ones I can't identify."

Tommy sipped his coffee, studied the screens, and listened. "JJ, what are your intentions? I know you won't let this go unchallenged. Neither would I. That said, I won't allow you to take matters into your own hands, like killing someone."

"I admit, I'm beyond angry with this jerk. I wouldn't take the law into my own hands unless I were physically threatened. I reacted. Now I want to find the creep and let you put 'em away."

Tommy nodded. "I'm here to get to the bottom of this mess. I respect your need to keep Jo safe. Please don't do anything I'd have to arrest you for, son. And yes, you can care for yourself using your martial arts skills."

JJ, frustrated, pounded the keyboard with the following program command. He faced Tommy and looked him in the eye. "I won't relax until the person is found. I'll turn over any valid evidence to you. Jo and I have so much emotional capital invested in Magnolia Bluff, but if she wakes up and tells me she wants to leave, we will. I won't stop looking."

Tommy set his coffee cup on the table and stared back. "If you stay, let me work it. You can be my shadow so I can keep an eye on you. I don't want text messages where you tell me to come to a new crime scene."

JJ stiffened, then looked at his clenched hands. "I'm waiting for the blackmailer to send instructions. I'll let you know."

Tommy growled. "My instincts tell me that leaving you alone is a poor idea."

The men jumped at the soft voice from behind. "It's okay, Tommy. JJ has me." Jo joined them and wrapped her arm around JJ's side. "I love our new home, and this person will not ruin it for us."

"Good. You have my number, Jo." Tommy shifted his eyes to JJ. "Don't get found anywhere at the wrong time. I can't unhear your threat from last night. Even though I kind of like and respect you, I will do my job."

"Thanks for coming by." JJ extended his hand to Tommy, and they shook.

Tommy was distracted as he drove towards Lily's Flower B&B. Parking, he reflected on the next steps for Jo's letter. "I've never heard of a blackmail case like this. I am unsure where to start, but Lily is one of the more friendly town gossips. She might have an idea. She knows Jo's identity and would protect that girl like a daughter. Time for another cup of coffee anyway."

Lily's face lit up when Tommy entered, making him feel welcome. He'd worried she might be too busy to chat. Her eyes went to the floor, and she shuffled her feet. "Is this a social call? Do you need a favor? Or am I in trouble again?"

Tommy laughed. "I needed that, Lily. I've got a problem, and I don't know where to start. You are one of the only people who might direct me."

Lily grinned. "I'm honored," she said, adding an almost curtsy. "That means two coffees, a seat in the back, and, based on the time of day, no bourbon. At least not for you. I don't recall ever being your go-to for help, but I'll grab the coffee, and you pick the table. We have at least thirty minutes before the customers arrive for breakfast. I have no guests, as my last one checked out two days ago. I heard he got a rental house from Joyce. It is a shame I can't keep this place filled year-round."

Lily turned and headed for the coffee. Tommy enjoyed her brew, which had less caffeine than JJ's. When Lily returned, she set the tray on the table. It contained cups, a coffee pot, and a small plate of sweet rolls.

"Renata is at school. What's the problem?"

Tommy stared at his cup, stirring to help it cool. "What I'm about to tell you is not for your gossip tree. I trust you to honor that, Lily." He added a hard stare for emphasis. "After everyone left last night, Jo found a blackmail letter on the coffee table. The note stated that payment was required at some unspecified time in cryptocurrency, or everybody in this hemisphere would know Jo's a supermodel from Brazil."

"What?" Lily sputtered, nearly spraying out the most recent sip. "Oh, that poor girl. I bet JJ is pissed."

Tommy held up his palm to continue. "I want to catch this person and put an end to it. Honestly, I don't know where to begin. I was hoping you might have some ideas on strangers in town bragging about skills, trying to pay for breakfast with crypto, wild bragging about JJ and Jo, or their housewarming party."

Lily rested her chin on her knuckles, her elbows on the table. He could almost see thoughts flashing across her mind.

"This town loves those two kids, Tommy. Anyone living here a year or more wouldn't do such a thing. I agree on new residents, but it could be anyone visiting. My guest rooms are vacant, but the person could stay in one of the cabins by the lake, which has good Wi-Fi. Or even the campgrounds. Summer brings lots of tourists and visitors to town."

"You mentioned the note found in the living room. That must mean the culprit was at the party. I was busy most of the event. I don't remember any strangers. There were quite a few people I hadn't seen in ages. I didn't spend much time in the house, though. Jason did, but he hasn't been here long enough to know regulars."

Tommy popped his neck from side to side. "I can learn who had water, trash removal, and electricity ordered in their name in the last few weeks. It would have been in the last month if they were new unless they've been biding their time until the kids returned."

"The party idea only started when they got here three weeks ago. Jo mentioned it when Joyce, Ann, Hank, Jason, and I went to help them unpack the mountain of boxes," reminded Lily.

"I can do background checks on new folks relatively easily if they applied for services. I'm sure there's a way I can check for heavy network access, as I suspect they must use that for research. And I'd bet Jo may not be the only target on this blackmailer's radar."

"Wow, I like how you think, Tommy. Joyce can tell you who she has rented to and connect you with other realtors who rent property. She was hustling everyone last night looking for opportunities." Lily chuckled. "It seems Jason is growing, and she needs to buy clothes for school."

Tommy nodded and jotted down a note.

"Maybe a relatively young, bold guy, likely single, with lots of computer equipment. That should be easy to spot." Lily air-wiped her hands and stood to clear the table, hearing the front bell indicating guests were arriving.

"Remind me why I haven't hired you, Lily."

Lily smirked. "Because this is the only place where I'd bring you coffee. I'm just joking. Get going. I have a guest to serve. Let me know if I can do anything else as you start peeling back the case."

CHAPTER 5

Checking In

Joyce had invited Brandon for a substantial breakfast, so she woke early Monday to prepare it for him and Jason before beginning her busy day. She grinned as Brandon and Jason wolfed the pancakes, eggs, and bacon like they'd been starved for days. Max sat patiently, barely drooling, while his big chocolate eyes roved between the two guys, hoping for a mistake that would end on the floor. Joyce internally giggled, imagining the thoughts going through the Labrador's mind. Taking pity on the sweet, forlorn-looking pup, she fixed a pancake with butter and a few drops of syrup and set the plate on the floor. After two licks and a swallow, the plate was clean enough to return to the cabinet.

"Brandon," she asked, "are you sure you don't mind taking Jason to school today?"

Brandon looked at her while finishing his most recent chew and held out his drained coffee cup for a refill. He grinned. "No problem. I'll get him there in time to flirt with the school girls, watching him play second base."

Joyce noted the heat rising on Jason's cheeks.

Her son opted to change the subject. "It's been two days since the party at the Rodreguiz's. I'm sure everything is back in order; Jo is so organized. I need to check with JJ about whether he needs my help at their place while they are in town. I want to find out if he was happy with what I did over the summer with my caretaking duties. I could help with the fall planting."

"Joyce, how about I pick Jason up after baseball practice and take him to their house to discuss the details? You've been busy with people you've helped find homes to rent. I don't mind."

Joyce smiled, thinking how kind and thoughtful this man was. "Yes, please, that would be perfect. I'm so glad he was accepted to the Texas Babe Ruth Youth Baseball League. He wanted to focus on improving at second base." She looked at her watch and frowned. "If it's not too much trouble, can you two do the dishes and clean up? I have so much to do today."

Brandon stopped in mid-bite, stunned. His eyes crossed to Jason, who grinned.

"It's the price for a great pancake breakfast. I figured you wouldn't mind. Plus, thanks for helping. I usually get stuck doing everything myself."

Joyce laughed at Brandon's sullen look. She kissed each of them on the cheek before grabbing her phone, purse, and keys. "See you later," she said before bolting out the door to her car.

Joyce meandered through her favorite well-maintained residential area, looking for any signs for sale or rental she could exploit. Her stomach clenched as she recalled how she and Jason nearly starved the first six months after relocating to Magnolia Bluff. It was more challenging than anticipated to establish herself as the go-to person for real estate anything in their new hometown. She wasn't shy about talking to strangers or encouraging homeowners to list their property with her. Folks said she knew how to earn their business without abrasive or smothering behavior, plus she was receiving referrals.

Hickory Street called her to turn as it was teaming with potential business. Recently, she'd had success with several for sale or rent, especially with summer nearing its end. Cruising slowly down the street, she spotted the wide-open front door of the rent-to-own houses she had closed on a couple of weeks ago. No one appeared out and about, though multiple cars were in the driveway. She stopped her car and grabbed her tablet to refresh her memory of the new tenant. Pulling up the information on the address, she found Adam Rawley had signed the lease. The notes contained a comment regarding his need for reliable internet service as he worked from home.

"The man paid two months in advance," she mumbled. "He was dowdy and rumpled, as I recall. It looks like he mowed the yard or called the lawn service I recommended." Looking around the quiet neighborhood, she decided no one was outdoors. Folks were either gone to work or, like Rawley, working from home. There was no rain in the forecast, but checking to see if he was home and closing the door seemed prudent.

Turning off the engine, she slipped the keys into her purse and headed toward the door, casually adjusting her flower-print dress. Joyce paused on the porch and called, "Mr. Rawley, it's Joyce, your realtor. I thought I'd stop by to see how you are settling in."

Nothing. After waiting a few heartbeats but hearing nothing, she pressed the doorbell and knocked on the doorframe. Still, no sounds came from inside. Frowning, she entered quietly to avoid disturbing a conference call or a meeting with the owner of the extra car in the driveway. At first glance, the entry appeared tidy. She rolled her eyes and thought, *he isn't as messy as I figured.*

Wandering into the kitchen, she noted no coffee pot or lights on. It was deathly quiet as she headed down the hallway into the living room. Joyce stepped through the doorway and stopped. Bringing her hand to her mouth, she gasped, "What in heaven's name happened?" It appeared like the aftermath of a tornado. Broken dishes littered the floor, lamps were knocked over, chairs lay on their sides, glasses shattered, and debris was everywhere. Her eyes darted from one mess to another as she mentally assessed the damage. Overcome with the enormity of the destruction, she knew her heart had stopped when she saw Rawley splayed out by an overturned chair. She took a deep breath and steeled herself to move closer when she spotted another man facedown—neither moved. She was too terrified to touch either body. Her breathing became erratic, and her fingers tingled. Afraid she'd faint, Joyce straightened, then closed her eyes, inhaling deeply, then exhaling slowly to the count of ten, three times. She opened her eyes. Neither man appeared to be breathing. The second man had familiar hair. She gingerly stepped over the items on the floor and noticed the man's hands and wedding ring. It dawned on her that the ring belonged to JJ; she'd noticed it at the barbecue.

Joyce wanted to scream but only emitted a crackled screech. Help, she needed help. Dread gripped her legs, making them feel like spaghetti noodles. She reached for the tabletop for stability. Terror coursed through her body as she feared the worst for JJ. She reached the doorway and leaned against it. She took another slow step down the hallway toward the exit and fumbled to extract the phone from her purse.

Time slowed to a crawl as she edged toward the entryway, struggling to gain access to her device to make the 911 call. She looked around the room, becoming more alarmed at the terrifying sights. As if underwater, Joyce heard the dispatcher when he answered, "911—What's your emergency?"

Inching down the hallway in a broken whisper, she begged, "Send the police; I think they're dead! 5678 Hickory Street." Not hearing the response, she released the phone and crumpled onto the floor into the welcoming darkness.

CHAPTER 6

An Unexpected Day

Joyce's brain registered a distant, unfamiliar voice calling her name. The words were garbled, like someone speaking from far away. Her body was comforted in a warm covering.

"Joyce, Miss Blackstone, Ma'am. I'm Steve. Can you open your eyes for me?"

The voice was calm but insistent, so she tried vainly to assemble her memories and figure out why someone named Steve would be speaking to her. She squinted her eyes in the dim light.

"Where," her fractured voice asked in a low whisper, "am I?" She could almost make out the unfamiliar yet pleasant face.

"You're in an ambulance, Joyce. I placed a warm blanket on you. You fainted, and I carried you here."

Joyce nodded, still confused about the why, but she wasn't afraid. Steve inserted the ear tips of the device into his ears. She felt the blood pressure cuff tighten on her arm as the cold disk of the stethoscope pressed against her skin.

Steve smiled. "You're doing great. Would you like to sit and have some water?"

Joyce tried to clear her throat of its scratchiness but moved as he propped his hand on her back. She sipped water from the cup and swallowed.

"More?"

Joyce shook her head no. She said, "Thank you," in her mind but heard no voice and only grunts for words.

"I am adept at lip reading, Ma'am. You're welcome. Take another sip, please." Steve called, "Tommy, she's awake."

Joyce focused on Tommy as he approached the back of the vehicle. She felt relieved but couldn't recall why.

Tommy helped her move to the edge of the ambulance's double back door opening. "Joyce, glad you're back with us. Are you up to answering a few questions?"

She half-smiled at Tommy, then looked around at the other officers talking near the front of the rental house. She spotted a gurney with a covered body and stared. Jumbled images rushed into her mind. Her eyes returned to Tommy, and she tried to speak. Her words came out as broken, unidentifiable sounds. Desperately, she gripped Tommy's arm and mumbled.

After a few frustrating minutes, tears spilled down her cheeks. She heard doors close and a vehicle making a strident siren sound moving away.

Tommy patted her arm. "I know you're trying to tell me what you saw in the Hickory Steet house. Let's not push too hard, Joyce."

Terror raced through her body, and the cup fell to the ground. She pressed her hands to her face and sobbed.

Tommy breathed a deep sigh. He patted her for reassurance. "You came to this house and saw something. We'll talk later after you've had time to rest. I'll have Steve and his buddy transport you to the hospital to let the docs check you over."

Joyce looked through her swollen eyes at Tommy. Her cracked whisper said, "Saw JJ."

Tommy nodded. "JJ was taken to the hospital. After the doctors check you and give me the okay, I will speak to you there."

Joyce felt light-headed and leaned against Steve's hand on her back.

"Tommy, she's going to black out again. She's shaking like crazy. The emotional trauma is too much for her." He scooted her back fully onto the gurney and covered her with a warm blanket.

The warmth felt inviting to Joyce. Her ears strained to hear more. She rested her eyes and listened to the click of a seat belt.

She heard Steve. "Tommy, we'll take care of her. I'll tell the staff to alert you when she's stable. It doesn't appear like she has any broken bones or bruises, but they'll do a full scan. There's no way to know if she was running or walking out, with her body half in and out of the house."

She heard concern in Tommy's response. "I've got nothing but questions. One dead, one unconscious and my witness isn't unstable. At least JJ's alive."

Joyce surrendered to the darkness with hope in her heart and the images retreating to the corners of her mind.

Tommy shook his head as he watched the ambulance pull away, waiting for the coroner to finish. "What a mess," he mumbled while he tried to decide who to call first. "Brandon needs to know about Joyce, plus he can grab Jason. He might have a good perspective on this crime with his background." Shifting his hat, he chewed his bottom lip. "What will I say to Jo without conveying my anger?"

Jake, the coroner, hollered, "When you have a minute, Chief, I need you in here."

Tommy strode into the house and followed Jake to the body. Reece Sovern, ex-military, recently promoted, heavy-set investigator, rolled his unlit cigar from one side of his mouth to the other before acknowledging Tommy with a nod. Reece tugged at his tie to loosen it as he gruffly interjected, "I have the outline of his form done and most of the area from the entrance to this spot filmed. If you're ready to transport, I've taken fingerprints in various places, as you can see by the dust, labeled based on the markers, and photographed each area. I can work on the rest of the evidence gathering…"

Tommy put his hand up to stop Reece from continuing. Reece returned a soured expression but held his tongue. "Jake, tell us what you have so far," said Tommy.

Jake sensed the tension and quickly replied, "Here's what I know. The deceased had his neck broken. It appears he was worked over pretty thoroughly before then. I need to bag his hands and then transport him to do a full autopsy. I will inventory everything on the body in my recording and report. I can begin that process when I get him on my table."

Tommy looked at the outline of where JJ was found and growled, "Like someone who was a martial arts expert?"

Jake shrugged. "Possibly. I don't know enough yet. The victim's hands are bloodied but may contain some trace evidence. My job is to provide facts. Based on the bruising, he was beaten before his neck was broken. I'll know more about the internal injuries after my exam."

"What about the other man? Do you have any insight into what happened to him?" Tommy asked.

"No, I overheard his EMT team say his knuckles were skinned, and he, too, was beaten. It could be they beat each other, and one lost. He had a handful of hair that Reece bagged as evidence. I asked the EMTs to bag his hands so the doctors could get any other evidence from under his nails."

Reece snarled, "Jake, was it Rawley's hair?"

"I've got samples of both men's hair and a portion of what JJ had in his hand to analyze. But I can't say for certain at this point."

"Can you tell how the victim's neck was broken?" Tommy asked.

Jake snorted, "You're asking me to speculate again. Let me do some analysis, then I can provide some facts."

Tommy grumbled, "All right, Jake, have it your way. Reece, you can go to the autopsy. Help Jake load the victim onto his gurney. I'm gonna take another look around before sealing off the house. We'll get the vehicles in the driveway transported to the city garage to check for evidence. Then I'll start making calls."

Tommy wandered through the house while the body was removed. He returned to the combined den and living room area, where broken items were strewn everywhere. He captured photos of the body outlines and ended up at a desk work area. Several Bitcoin doodles with random notes scattered about were visible. A group of letters caught Tommy's attention. JoW was heavily traced and appeared retraced on the pad. His shoulders slumped, and he closed his eyes, sensing the limited options that would drive this investigation.

Reece appeared at Tommy's side, reading over his shoulder.

Tommy sighed and faced Reece. "This may answer why JJ was here."

Reece appeared puzzled.

"It can't be a coincidence that her initials are scribbled on this notepad," affirmed Tommy. "I'm afraid Rawley wrote the blackmail letter I brought marked as evidence to check for finger-prints from Jo and JJ's party."

"It looks like JJ found the blackmailer ahead of us," Reece suggested, "and came to reason with him."

Tommy momentarily glared at Reece, then bagged the notepad, labeling it as evidence. "Lock this place up," he said before he turned and left.

CHAPTER 7

Help is on the Way

The late morning call to Brandon's cell phone made him grin. "Joyce's dishwasher, Jason's driver, and new squeeze here. How's it going, honey?"

There was a short pause before a soft woman's voice replied, "Is this Brandon?"

"Yes."

"This is Claire, a hospital nurse, calling from Joyce's phone. Sorry for the confusion. Your name is tagged as her favorite contact, and she told me to call you."

Several emotions raced through Brandon as he gripped the phone tighter. "Why are you using Joyce's phone? What happened? Where is she?"

"Joyce is in the emergency room at the hospital," Claire soothed. "She is physically fine but is having a few issues resulting from shock. If you can join her, it might help. How soon could you get here?"

Brandon ran his hand through his hair, then grabbed his keys off the counter. "I'm on my way, ma'am."

Tommy stored his sunglasses in his pocket, straightened his hat, and knocked smartly on the front door. A moment later, he pressed the doorbell.

Jo stared in surprise as she opened it, wiping her hands with a kitchen towel. "Tommy, you could have come through the side door from the pergola. You're like family. JJ's out and about, but I expect him soon. What's up?"

Tommy took a deep breath, focusing on Jo's beautiful expresso-colored eyes. He felt less than family-like at this moment. "JJ is why I'm here. Since he was driving your rental, I thought I'd give you a lift."

Jo's eyes widened. "Come in, Tommy." She tugged at his sleeve, pulled him into the house, and shut the door. "Was driving? Was he in an accident?"

"Jo," seeing the fear in her eyes, he realized this would be a tough conversation. "There was an incident. I need you to come to the hospital with me now, please."

Jo froze with her mouth open, unable to respond.

Tommy touched her shoulder to help steady her. "I didn't want just to call because…it wouldn't be fair to tell you that way. JJ is in the hospital. The rental is in temporary impound pending the investigation. Get your phone and purse. I'll take you now. We can discuss more later."

Tommy watched her grasp his words.

Almost mechanically, she replied, "Yes, of course." She held out one hand and counted the tasks. "I'll lock the front door. My phone is on the charger in the kitchen, and my purse is in the bedroom. I'll get a sweater, as hospitals are always cold." She sucked in a breath. "I won't cry now, but don't touch me, Tommy; I'll lose control. I can't lose control if JJ needs me."

Tommy quietly stated, "Okay. Get your things and bring something to take notes on. There will be lots of information you'll need to track. One step at a time."

Jo nodded and held up her chin as she rushed around, picking up the items with Tommy on her heels. She took a quick look around the kitchen and touched off the lights. She set the alarm by the side door, which Tommy opened for her to leave. They headed to his vehicle, and he guided her into the passenger door like a gentleman.

Tommy settled into the driver's seat, started the engine, and asked, "Are you doing all right?"

"No. I want to know what happened and how he's doing."

"I honestly don't know exactly what happened. He was alive but unconscious when taken to the hospital. That's all I know. I'm not a doctor."

Jo stared straight ahead. "This is the portion of my vows where I agreed, from this day forward, for better, for worse, for richer, for poorer, in sickness and in health, to love and to cherish, till death do us part. He's alive. That is ALL that matters right now, Tommy."

He put the car into gear, accelerated, and guided it to the highway toward the hospital. "Mrs. Rodreguiz, he's gonna need you to stay strong. He always brags about you. You've shown your strength before. Let's go see a man about a problem."

Tommy noted the determination on her face and clasped hands as he hit the siren.

CHAPTER 8

When is Timing Ever Good?

Based on his former career in the New York Police Department Narcotics Division, Brandon was no stranger to hospitals. This time was to see someone special, a person he cared about and wanted in his life. He entered the emergency area with focused determination and indexed various questions and scenarios in his mind. He clenched his jaw and rocked his neck from side to side to relieve the tension that had persisted since Claire's call about Joyce. Over the years, he'd seen the worst of humanity, but today, he felt more vulnerable than when guys had aimed guns or knives at him. Caring had changed him. He strode in the directions the signs pointed to, checking the door numbers for his target. He missed seeing Jo and Tommy lingering at the nurse's station.

"Brandon," a soft feminine voice called.

Then, a man said, "Hey, Brandon."

Brandon stopped and turned toward the sounds. "I didn't see you guys. The hospital called me. I'm worried sick about why Joyce couldn't call me herself. What are you two doing here?"

He noticed Jo appeared a bit smaller with no smile, which was unusual.

She took a ragged breath but said nothing.

Tommy looked straight at him. "Jo is waiting on JJ's status. He was brought in by ambulance a while ago. The nurse is checking to see if Jo can see him.

"Oh, Jo. I'm sorry. What happened?"

Tommy moved his head slightly and frowned. "We're getting his status."

Not missing the silent demand to let it go, Brandon said, "I hope he's okay, Jo. I need to find Joyce. I'll be here if you need anything."

Tommy held Brandon's arm and eased him to the side out of Jo's earshot. Tommy softly said, "If she's speaking, come find me."

Brandon's detective brain jumped into high alert. The hair on his arm raised. "Why would you need to speak with Joyce, Chief?"

Tommy shrugged. Brandon followed the man's eyes as he glanced at Jo.

Tommy cleared his throat. "She may have some information, is all. Right now, I need to help Jo get the status on JJ. I'll find you before I leave, promise," he quietly stated.

Brandon, confused, noticed activity behind the counter of the nurse's station. "Hopefully, this is good news for you, Jo. I need to find Joyce's room. We'll talk later, Chief."

Brandon turned to head down the quiet hallway and heard, "Mrs. Rodreguiz, your husband is being evaluated. Please have a seat. We'll let you know when you can see him."

Brandon's mind picked apart the new information while he walked. JJ was being evaluated, but for what? At least he wasn't in surgery. Joyce wasn't speaking, but Tommy wanted to talk to her. He stopped by a nurse working on a chart leaning against a wall. "Excuse me, ma'am. Can you point me to Room F?"

She smiled. "Yes. Take a right at the next opening, and it's the second door down on the left."

"Thank you," he said, then quickened his step. Relief swept through him as he walked into the room and saw her sitting up with no bandages.

CHAPTER 9

Just Facts, But Not All

Tommy leaned against the hospital wall, wishing he could turn back time. His mind raced through the sights and information at the Hickory Street house. He periodically glanced at Jo as she fidgeted in her chair and wrung her hands, waiting for JJ's status. His thoughts were interrupted by a commotion at the nurse's station. He heard,

"Sir, you're not on the list," a nurse said. "The police have this area cordoned off. You can't…"

The man barreled past and made a beeline towards Tommy. He brazenly stopped and tilted his head to look into Tommy's face. The man's white short-sleeved shirt, untucked from khaki slacks, showed a hint of sweat, suggesting the mid-day heat was at fault. "Chief Jager, I'm Landon Pace, a freelance reporter for the Magnolia Bluff Chronicle. Graham sent me. I heard the police and EMS radio chatter earlier. I need information to fill in the blanks. Graham wants to get this story on the cover of the next edition."

Tommy adjusted his Stetson to formal status and straightened. Without a word, he grabbed the man under his left arm and escorted him from the immediate area.

Tommy stopped in a quiet area of an alcove beside the elevators. "You had better get what I'm going to tell you exactly right for your publication. Otherwise, it'll be the last scoop you ever get. Explain that to Graham, or I will find a cell for you in the county jail."

Landon swallowed hard but, to his credit, didn't back down. "Chief, I've got a job to do just like you. People need to know the goings-on in their community. I am obliged to report it." He removed a notepad and pencil from his pocket and poised it over the paper as he continued, "Now some dead guy and the nearly dead guy…"

Tommy stepped forward, which caused the man to get pressed against the wall. "I've got an investigation with lots of missing answers. I don't need you to do cowboy reporting and mess up my case. I'll tell you what you can say. If you add any speculation, gossip, or hearsay to the print copy, you'll be arrested for obstructing my investigation. I don't want any embellishment. Do you understand?"

Landon nervously nodded. He scribbled while Tommy dictated.

"A community member dropped by a new neighbor's house to see how he was getting on. The individual found two men unconscious after what looked like a very spirited discussion that involved a fight. One man was pronounced dead at the scene and taken by the coroner; the other was rushed to the hospital. The man is in critical condition and unable to provide a statement to authorities at this time. No names will be released until the next of kin are advised."

Landon frowned at the skimpy information. "This isn't enough, Chief. What about the emergency teams providing prompt care? Who was the community member?"

"The individual who found the men was traumatized. The family requested the name be withheld for the time being." Tommy used his index finger to tap the man's chest. "We don't want to cause a rush of people to bother a responsible citizen before they can rest, right? Once I have this crime scene solved, you can get the exclusive. I will dole out some additional details to allow follow-up articles directly to you. You help me, and I'll give you credit. Best I got, Landon."

Landon brightened. "Thanks, Chief. I'm happy to assist. I'll await your call."

CHAPTER 10

We're Judgmental— Sometimes of Ourselves

Brandon rushed to Joyce's bedside, ignoring the nurse. She stared blankly into space. "Honey, I'm here." He took her hand as she nodded, and her face softened.

The nurse smiled. "You must be Brandon. I'm Claire. Joyce is doing fine but has suffered some emotional trauma. Now that you're here, let me get the doctor to explain the situation. Joyce has already signed approval to give you information about her medical condition. She's getting some hydration with the IV, but nothing serious." Claire patted Joyce's hand. "The doctor will be in soon. Use the pad and paper to communicate, ma'am."

Joyce nodded and picked up the yellow tablet and pencil from her lap.

Brandon, she wrote, *things are mixed up. I fainted—more than once. My throat is scratchy. I can't talk.*

"It's okay. We'll figure it out. Let's listen to the doctor's orders and find out when I can get you home." He looked at his watch. "Jason is at school. The coach takes them to ball practice. If you aren't released, I'll get him and bring him here."

Joyce gave a half smile.

He stroked her hand and then brushed back a bit of her hair with his fingertips. "Do you hurt anywhere?"

She shook her head.

"Did you get into a car accident?"

Her mouth formed a circle, and she shook her head.

"I ran into Tommy and Jo on my way to find you," Brandon said. "Jo is waiting to find out when she can see JJ."

Joyce closed her eyes, and he noticed a bit of moisture forming on her lashes. She blinked rapidly and sighed with a slight smile.

She scribbled, *He's alive. That's great. I've been worried about the images in my mind.*

"You were with JJ?"

Joyce shrugged, her fists balled, and her left hand pounded the bed. She jotted; *I don't know. I was driving to work. I parked. Then I see pieces I can't put together. I'm scared.*

Hearing the door open, Brandon looked, seeing the doctor arrive with a patient chart and Claire on his heels.

"I'm Dr. Miles. You must be," he glanced at the chart, "Brandon Turner."

"Yes, sir."

"Miss Blackstone, the recent check on your vitals indicates everything on that front is good. When the IV is finished, we'll remove it." He checked her eyes with his small flashlight. "Do you have any pain?"

Joyce shook her head and grunted a short. "Naa."

Spotting the pad, he said, "Your voice hasn't returned, but you can communicate. Good. Do you recall what happened to you?"

She shook her head and pointed to the notepad area where she'd written to Brandon what she knew.

Dr. Miles read it and looked her in the eye. "Miss Blackstone, I believe you are in shock. In speaking with the police earlier, they told me you phoned 911. When the police arrived, they found you lying on the ground. The EMT attendant indicated you did black out twice before bringing you here. Claire has been beside you most of the time and indicated you have not fainted or lost consciousness since you arrived. At this point, you appear to have memory loss as a result of a trauma or shock, as there are no signs you were assaulted. I suspect this contributes to the lack of voice or hysterical aphonia in medical terms. Your condition should resolve with time and without medication, but it could last several days or weeks." He patted her arm. "With good rest and light activity, you'll wake one morning and sing in the shower." He made some notes on the chart and handed it to Claire. "Unless you feel the need to stay and enjoy our hospital food. I will discharge you into Mr. Turner's care for transport. Let him drive you around for a day or two. Please visit your doctor if you have any other symptoms, including lightheadedness."

Brandon squeezed her hand and released the breath he hadn't realized he'd been holding. Joyce almost smiled in agreement.

"Thank you, Doctor Miles," Brandon said. "I have no problem chauffeuring her."

"Take the notepad with you, Mrs. Blackstone, to communicate with people and to make notes as memories click into place."

She nodded and smiled. Joyce started to swing her legs to get up when Claire pressed a hand gently on her shoulder.

"Joyce, I need to get the discharge paperwork together for you. I will find a wheelchair to get you to the car." Looking at Brandon, she added, "Mr. Turner, if you want, you can pull your car around to the ER entrance and park. It's going to take some time to complete her release papers."

"Sounds like a plan." He leaned in and whispered to Joyce, "I'll be back shortly and take you home. You want me to call your office and tell them you'll be out for a few days?"

She nodded.

Brandon left the room with a lighter step than when he entered. He spotted Tommy outside another door, speaking to an officer and rotating his Stetson hat around by the brim.

Tommy looked up and approached him. "How's Joyce?"

Brandon frowned with a sense of concern washing over him. "Physically, she's fine. She called 911, according to the doctor. She was unconscious when police arrived. Where did you find her, Tommy?"

Tommy moved his mouth and eyes as if assessing how much to say. "She was lying on the open doorway at a home on Hickory Street. I called the EMT team as I didn't want to move her in case of hidden injuries. I checked her pulse, and she was breathing."

Brandon kept asking, as Tommy was not volunteering facts. "She wrote down a few details of driving to a house, though she didn't name the street. She's seeing flashes of unconnected images, like partial amnesia. She can't talk, and the doctor used a term associated with laryngitis. She somehow worried that JJ was dead. What aren't you telling me, Tommy?"

Tommy ground his teeth, appearing frustrated. Tommy pulled him into an empty room across the hallway and closed the door. "We found two bodies in the house. One was JJ, out cold. The other, we believe, is Adam Rawley, a new person in town to whom Joyce rented the house. He was dead. Joyce was sprawled on the doorstep but at one point called 911 for help, stating the address and saying, *I think they're dead.* With your background as a New York detective, I know you understand how to keep this quiet. Frankly, I don't have much to go on. One man is dead, another in a coma, and my only witness has a memory issue and problems communicating."

Brandon blinked, stunned. "Is JJ in the room across the hall? Does Jo know the circumstances?"

Tommy shook his head. "She knows he is injured and being evaluated. He's been beaten up and is visibly bruised. They're waiting on the results of the X-rays and other tests to decide the next treatment steps. Jo couldn't tell me why JJ left home without leaving a note or calling to say where he was going."

"Do you need me to help? I can drive her to her rental if you want," Brandon offered, mentally juggling the timing for commitments he'd already made.

"No, the rental is impounded, as is his cell phone, as part of the investigation. And I know she won't leave his side until the medical team insists."

Brandon looked at his watch, took a piece of paper and pen from his coat pocket, and wrote his number. "Here, call me if you need me to come get Jo. Joyce is being released, and then I need to pick up Jason from practice in a couple of hours. Is Joyce's car being held?"

"No," said Tommy, his tone growing agitated. "It's parked on Hickory Street. I locked it up before coming here. The keys are likely in Joyce's purse. I'll give Jo your number so she can call you when she needs to return home. I'll tell her as much as I can without compromising my investigation." Tommy finger-combed his hair.

Brandon appreciated the line Tommy was walking, even with the tiny bits of new information. "Good. I'll watch Joyce and let you know if she recalls anything new. I need to get my truck and take her home. Please keep me posted on JJ's condition."

Tommy nodded and shook his hand before they parted in the hallway.

CHAPTER 11

Strength When Needed

Distressed, Jo breathed shallowly while holding JJ's hand, thinking of things to talk with him about. The nurse told her that talking to him was good. She spoke of the chores completed and the flowers she planned to plant. Anything but asking what happened. Her fears were balanced like on a tightrope, listening to the sounds of the breathing tubes, praying they were helping. Beeps and chirps from the monitoring sensors attached to his body, plus the seesaw noise of the IV stuck into his arm, were making her fidgety. Combined, the sounds were a misbegotten symphony she couldn't stand listening to but didn't want to hear end until his eyes opened. Images of his sparring abilities and tender touches threatened to overcome her promise to be the strong one. She stroked his thumb with hers and whispered, "I love you, JJ. You're the strongest man I know. You can beat this and return to me for us."

The nurse returned to check on her patient. Jo ignored the nurse because, as they had discussed earlier, her chair was out of the way. A squealing alarm disrupted the familiar hums, making Jo jump.

"What's wrong?" she asked, knowing in her heart that everything was wrong.

The nurse smiled and reassuringly squeezed Jo's shoulder. "Relax. I'm changing his IV fluid, and the machine alerts me when something's disconnected. Even if I weren't here, someone at the station would know immediately. Your husband is strong, and his body is making him rest to help him recover. Some test results are in, so the doctor will be here soon to discuss the next steps."

Endless seconds, then minutes, ticked by. Jo's eyes darted to the door, willing it to open. The doctor entered with a chart in hand and an unreadable expression.

"Hello again. Your husband's vitals are good, and we are treating him to prevent brain swelling from the concussion. The MRI and X-rays showed us some treatment options. We have taped his broken ribs and will continue to help him breathe. His temperature is higher than we like, so we will monitor it and change medications. You did say he is on no standard medications, correct?"

"No, sir. He takes no medicine. As I mentioned, his regular doctor is in Brazil. I can reach out and get any medical history you want. I have waited to do that until I know what to convey to his regular doctor." Between ragged breaths, Jo added. "I feel helpless. I can't do anything to fix the situation or help him heal faster. Yesterday everything was wonderful. It changed in the blink of an eye. What do I do now?"

The doctor nodded. "He needs time to recover. We never know how long a person may remain in a coma. Your husband will be moved from here in Emergency to our ICU area. I know you want to be by his side, but the ICU visiting hours are restricted to thirty minutes, three times a day. At this point, he cannot travel or leave the hospital without a significant risk. Have your family doctor call, and I can fill in the details. Go home, take care of yourself, and let us care for him. You can contact the nurse's station anytime. We have your number. You will be advised if his condition changes. We have a great medical team here."

The doctor left. Then, as if on cue, an orderly and the nurse returned to transfer JJ. Jo leaned over and kissed his cheek. "I'll see you later, honey."

Standing up straight, saying prayers in her heart, she watched as they carefully arranged all the lines and support machines to exit the room, leaving her alone. Feeling numb, she gathered her purse and wrap.

Just then, Tommy entered. "Jo, I've spoken to Brandon. He said he could take you home whenever you want." He handed her the paper with Brandon's number while fidgeting with the brim of his Stetson.

Jo scrunched up her face, confused. "Why can't I just get the rental that JJ drove? I'm sure you know where it is. That way, I won't inconvenience anyone."

Tommy cleared his throat. "Jo, the car is impounded. Our team is checking it for evidence. Same with his cell phone. I'll get them to you when we are finished. He was found at the scene of a murder, next to the victim. We're investigating why he was there."

Standing straighter, with her chin out, feeling the anger rise, she said, "Why didn't you give me these details earlier? Does that mean JJ is a suspect? Tommy, you can't be serious."

"I'll have a man outside ICU until he regains consciousness," Tommy continued. "Until we get more answers, I must treat him like a suspect. The victim may be responsible for your blackmail note, but we're still gathering evidence."

Jo reeled from his late-coming information. She struggled to remain upright like he had yanked a rug from under her feet. Tommy reached to hold her, but she batted his hand. "Don't you touch me," she snapped. "You'd do this knowing JJ, and I helped you? This is how you treat him? I thought you were an honorable Texan, Chief."

Tommy looked at her with anger in his eyes. "I told JJ no cowboy antics and to call me with any leads. So, what does he do? I find him, possibly at the blackmailer's house, with a man dead next to him. They looked like they'd had a knockdown drag-out fight, with JJ the winner in the end. With no eyewitnesses to say otherwise, your husband is suspect number one."

The truth of the crime scene sank into Jo. Closing her eyes, she shook her head. "I understand, Tommy. JJ said he was going to kill the blackmailer."

Tommy took a breath. "No matter what I think or feel for you and JJ, this is police protocol. I will follow the evidence and turn over every rock in the way. Please, share anything you find because I know you'll look, and Brandon could help."

Jo looked up with tears threatening to spill. "I know where to start."

"The nurse said it would take a while, but sheesh," Brandon groused. "How long does it take to mark on a chart *Alice doesn't live here anymore*?" After ten minutes of pacing by the side of the truck, the glass doors slid open, revealing Claire pushing Joyce in the wheelchair toward him. Joyce's fingers wiggled a wave, and her face lit up. Joyce was shaky as she stood, so Brandon guided her into the front seat without bonking her head. He placed her purse and the notepad in her lap. Joyce fastened the seat belt, and then he closed the door. He rushed to the driver's side, entered the four-seater pickup, and started the engine.

"Are you ready to get home?"

She nodded with a smile, adding a thumbs-up with her right hand.

Elated to take her home, he began a stream of storytelling about Max's antics for the short drive, hoping it would help her relax. She attempted some giggles. He noticed her lips rise, and then she resumed staring out the side window as if searching for answers.

Brandon changed tactics. "Jason's baseball practice is nearly over. Would you like to go with me or have me drop you off at the house and go get him?"

A panicked look enveloped her face. She grabbed the notepad and pen and then scribbled. *Don't let him see me like this!*

Brandon rocked his head and chin, surprised. "All right. I'll drop you off so you can get settled. I'll explain to him what happened so we aren't springing this on him all at once. I'll take him to your Camry and follow him back to the house. Is that okay with you?"

Joyce nodded her assent, her eyes less fearful than moments before.

Brandon teased, "Once we arrive, how about I take you to bed?" He enjoyed the priceless look on her face. "Kidding, but you can file it under things to do later. I'll take you to your room. No trying to fix supper or marathon housecleaning. I'll order some food for dinner. Think about what you'd enjoy while I'm gone."

Joyce grinned and wrote something, then scratched it out. She sighed.

CHAPTER 12

Make a List

Jo huffed aloud as she pushed the door open and left the room. Without access to JJ, she needed to pull herself together. Pacing down the hallway for what seemed forever, she spotted the sign Welcome Multifaith Space. Opening the door, she entered, glad it was unoccupied. She spotted signs of various religious beliefs, including stained glass scenes, crosses, and the Star of David, undoubtedly used to give individuals a place to reflect or pray. The muted colors of the furnishings and the low hum of white noise were calming. She sank into a chair with a comfy cushion, organizing her thoughts, terrified her husband might not make it. She pulled out her cell, pressing the sequence JJ had taught her—the call connected.

"Hi, Jo," Brayson answered. "How can I help you? I'm still working on finding some additional information for JJ."

"Brayson…" She wrapped her free arm around her slim waist. "JJ is in the hospital. He's suffered a horrific beating with broken ribs, along with a couple of damaged knuckles, stitches, and a concussion resulting in a coma."

"I'm pinging your location at the county hospital outside Magnolia Bluff."

"Yes, that's where we are. They recently moved him into an open bed in the ICU, so I can't be with him the whole time." She sniffled. "I'm not certain what to do."

"I can arrange for a medical transport…"

"No," she said. "He can't be moved. The doctor told me that specifically due to the possibility of brain swelling." She turned her phone and snapped a photo of the doctor's business card. "Any doctor I say can confer with the doctor here."

"Got it. Do you need me to catch a flight to be with you or any of the family? I can get a hold of them on your behalf."

Jo closed her eyes and inhaled. "Brayson, you must have spoken with him earlier. Something caused him to leave our home and go across town. Did he message you that he'd found something?"

"No. At five-something your time this morning, he gave me the list of the guests who RSVPed via email and the video capture files. I'm finding driver's licenses or other public photos to cross-match. I'm working to verify the faces between those two sources. It will take longer to match even with our computer power. No outliers yet on that search."

"Oh, Brayson," she moaned. "He left before I awoke. He didn't leave a note. His computer was still on, but not where I could log in to see what he'd been doing. I started on other chores, so I didn't bother touching it. Tommy told me JJ was found in the house rented to a man who may have been the blackmailer. JJ was lying on the floor, beaten and unconscious, while the other man was dead. Please don't tell the family yet."

Jo heard Brayson's hand hitting something with a bang. He loudly inhaled. "I don't like it, Jo. I can get on a flight."

She struggled with the options, not wanting to create a circus media event in town. "I was hoping you could get a doctor you trust to get all the information on JJ and to be a remote consultant on his care. Then I'll call his parents and reassure them there is nothing they can do here. They are on their first vacation in ten years. I don't want them here to visit for a few minutes each day." Jo sniffled and dabbed her eyes. "You can access JJ's phone and PC for anything new. There is an ex-New York detective in town, Brandon Turner, who Tommy said could drive me home from the hospital and maybe help put things together."

"Why can't you just take the rental car?"

She nodded her head and smacked her mouth. "The car and his phone are with the police as evidence. He is under guard in the ICU. It's a mess, and I'm shaking like a leaf."

Brayson chuckled. "You may be shaking, Jo, but you're taking the right steps by calling me. JJ will be proud when he wakes up. I'll review his phone data and see what other information I can tap into. They may have it, but I have access to it. We can speak after you get home. I bet you're tired and probably haven't eaten."

"I could use some food," she admitted. "But you know the worst part, Brayson?"

"I thought I heard all the worst parts."

"Nope. I'm to blame for him being in the hospital."

"How do you figure that?"

She sighed, and tears welled in her eyes. "I wouldn't let him set a video camera in the living room where we could have captured the face of the blackmailer and let Tommy deal with it. JJ let me have my way." The tears rolled down her cheeks.

"Jo, don't think that. You're not to blame. JJ would be crushed if he knew you thought that. So, stop. Let's see what we can find out. Perhaps Mr. Turner, who has a stellar record from what I see here, could be a great asset. I hear your sobs. Dry your eyes, call your ride, and walk out with your head held high."

Between blowing her nose and gulping air, she said, "Thank you, Brayson,"

"We'll talk later. Check in if you need anything."

Jo left the Multifaith Room and entered the nearest restroom to take a health break and wash her face. Cool paper towels on her eyes reduced the swelling. Thankfully, she hadn't applied makeup this morning.

She exited the women's room and walked but felt lost. She stopped a man dressed in hospital scrubs. "I got turned around. Can you point me to the Emergency Room exit, please?"

The man appeared stunned. "You must have been walking quite a while. Come with me, and I'll get you most of the way there. I'll show you where to turn right, and you'll be out in no time."

"Thank you." She turned and walked beside him, making small talk. She learned he was a phlebotomist, which struck her as fascinating, so she asked many questions.

They reached the intersection and stopped. "This is where we part company," he said. "I get off at seven if you'd like to go for a bite to eat."

Flattered and slightly lighter, she replied, "Thank you. But my husband, even in a coma here, wouldn't approve."

The man looked at her empathetically. "I'm sorry to hear he's ill, and I wish you both well. Take a right, and you'll be outside in under five minutes."

"Thank you."

Jo found her way to the exit without having to see Tommy. She walked into the bright sun and fished her sunglasses from her purse. Pushing her worry aside, she embraced the warmth of Texas in the late afternoon. Finding a bench in the shade, she sat down and wrote a list of things to do.

CHAPTER 13

Bad Days Are What You Make of Them

Brandon stopped at his place and picked up Max. Then he drove Joyce home, leaving the dog to keep her company. Joyce brightened, and Max was all about getting lavished with petting.

"Joyce, Max can stay with you while I get Jason. I can fix you a cup of tea and maybe make you a late lunch before I leave."

Joyce nodded and scribbled a note. *Thanks, I am hungry. Can you also get me some treats from the pantry to share with Max?*

"Of course." He made her a ham and cheese sandwich with lettuce and tomato. He set some chips on the side and a few cookies for later while the water boiled. He filled the mug with boiling water and an Earl Grey tea bag to steep. Grabbing a few dog treats, he set that plate on the table with Max following his every movement. "He won't let you forget about his treats; I promise."

Joyce's voice crackled as she tried to chuckle and patted Max's head.

Brandon checked his watch. "I need to head to the practice field, but I'll be back after I've explained things to him." He scratched Max. "Be a good boy."

The pickup started right away, and Brandon headed toward the baseball fields. The kids had finished gathering their stuff when he stopped the car. The coach said Jason improved with each practice and discussed the upcoming game.

He reached his arm around Jason as they walked to the truck. "Coach said you're doing great," he said.

"I like playing ball a lot. I'm starting for the game next week. It's good."

They reached his vehicle, and Jason threw his gear into the truck bed.

Brandon stopped. "Jason, there was an incident this morning, and your mom ended up in the hospital."

Jason's face turned to a sickly green with a slice of fear.

"She's fine, buddy, and at home. She wasn't physically hurt but has lost her voice and a portion of her memory."

Jason let out a breath. "You promise she's not injured?"

"Yes!" He nodded. "Her memory and voice will come back in just a few days. Max is keeping her company."

Jason nodded. "Okay."

"We need to retrieve her car from a house on Hickory Street. Would you mind driving it home?" he added with a smile.

Jason's eyes got huge. Brandon swore the youth grew an inch in that moment. "Heck, yeah. I meant, yes, sir, I can do that."

"Great, I knew I could count on you." They did a high-five and got into his pickup.

Fifteen minutes later, Brandon pulled behind Joyce's vehicle and parked. He handed Jason the keys. "I'll follow you, son." Clapping him on the shoulder, he teased, "Hey, no doing donuts in your mom's car."

Jason held up his hand in mock innocence and chuckled. He glanced toward the house. "What's up with the yellow tape over the door? Was mom at a crime scene and screamed at someone for trampling the yard? She yelled so loud and long that she lost her voice."

Brandon kicked himself for not considering the telltale markings in the aftermath of the crime. "Yes, it's a crime scene. Police think she may have seen something, but she can't recall. If you're alone with her later and she says things, try to write them down, but let's keep it in the family. We don't need to fuel any gossip."

"Okay. Wow, Mom might have seen something." Jason got in the car. It started immediately. He carefully eased onto the street toward the house with Brandon right behind.

Arriving at Joyce's home, Jason pulled into the driveway to park while Brandon pulled in behind him. Jason grabbed his gear from the pickup, and they headed inside. Max made a beeline for Jason with slobbering licks.

Brandon, followed by Jason and Max, found Joyce sitting in the kitchen with hot tea and wearing a pink lounging outfit. The coloring of her cheeks looked better. "I see you changed. Any issues?"

Joyce smiled but shook her head. She garbled a "Haa ss."

Jason's face shifted to concern. "Mom, Brandon told me what happened. Does it hurt?"

She scribbled on the pad. *No, but it's frustrating.*

Jason hip-bumped Brandon and grinned. "I guess she can't tell me to do any chores for a while."

Joyce glared at her son.

Brandon put up his hand. "Don't pick on your mother, Jason. She can scribble fast; you might get extra chores with any backtalk."

They laughed. Brandon's phone rang, and he accepted.

"Hello…Oh, hi, Jo…Sure, I can do that." He looked around. "Your timing's good…I can leave Joyce's in the next ten minutes to come there…Great, see you soon."

Joyce and Jason stared at him as he turned around. "That was Jo. She needed a ride home from the hospital, and I had volunteered to help. I hope you don't mind, Joyce."

Brandon spotted the worry in her eyes. He stroked her shoulder reassuringly. "JJ's been transferred into the ICU. She's not permitted to sit by him for more than thirty minutes at a time. It's all good."

Joyce sighed and nodded, then wrote. *Take as long as you need. I'll be fine.*

Brandon handed Jason some cash. "How about you order some food?"

"No problem. We'll be fine." He sat in an adjacent chair. Max placed his head on Jason's lap. "Besides, Max is here too."

"Okay, see you later." He kissed the top of Joyce's head and gently squeezed her shoulder before returning to his truck.

He pulled through the driving circle by the ER door. He muttered, "Much more of this, and I'll ask for a frequent parker sign for the truck."

Jo waved. She walked to the passenger side.

Brandon grinned. "I'll bet JJ is the kind of husband who opens the door for you. Am I right?"

Seeing her face pale, he hastily offered, "I'm sorry, but I thought a little levity might cut the tension."

She settled in and fastened the safety belt. "It's been a bad day, Brandon. I understand Joyce was mixed up in this mess, so I suspect your day wasn't much better. How's she doing?"

Brandon sighed. "First, it was trying to figure out what was happening with her. Then I had to explain it, at least what I know, to Jason. He's with her now, ordering dinner to be delivered."

"How did Jason deal with it? He's been a great caretaker to our property while we were away working."

"He stepped in and even drove her car home. I parked Max at her house while I came to get you. He's a wonderful distraction, grubbing for affection to help take her mind off the incident."

"At least you have mobility," Jo complained. "I'll have to pester people for rides back and forth to the hospital because Tommy impounded our rental."

Brandon shrugged. "Yeah, I know. Everyone was dealt a lousy scenario today. Tommy thinks Joyce stumbled into the house, and something happened there that affected her memory. She has a form of laryngitis. According to what she has told us in notes, she recalls disjointed flashes but nothing specific."

Jo exhaled. "You're an ex-police detective. You look at all this as a case. Lucky you. My husband's lying in a coma, and as soon as he wakes up, Tommy's going to throw him in jail as a murder suspect. I've had some rotten days, but this one beats my worst by a mile."

Brandon caught the abrupt shift in her conversation and glanced at her, trying to decide what to say next. "Ms. Rodreguiz, it occurs to me that everyone has questions, including the police, on this issue. We have important people in our lives who are in this hot mess. Tommy groused that he didn't have much to go on. What if you and I work together to get more answers?"

Jo seemed to study the offer for a minute and pick it apart. "I'm not sure that's a good idea. We'd need to share information to make a partnership work. JJ and I are very private people. We moved here to retain our privacy."

Brandon frowned at Jo. "Are you afraid I'd find out you're the fabulous international model JoW of Destiny Fashions?"

Jo's eyes widened, utterly surprised, and fear crossed her face.

"Names and faces were my specialty in the NYPD," he added, "as well as keeping confidential information."

Jo closed her eyes and let her head slump forward, then asked, "Tommy told you?"

Brandon laughed. "No, he's cut from the same cloth as me for keeping confidences. Your lovely face has graced Times Square more than once. I didn't need to verify by searching the internet, which would have been a cinch. Anyone could if they had an inkling." He started the truck. "My first guess is that our dead guy found you online. Instead of respecting your privacy, he was probably trying to blackmail you. JJ was smart enough to figure out who it was, so he confronted him. But I haven't seen all the evidence—those are assumptions on my part."

Jo straightened up and drew a halting breath. "Brandon, I could use your help. I need to exonerate JJ." Her fists clenched. "No matter how mad he was, he wouldn't go to kill anyone."

Brandon chuckled. "I like your devotion. Everyone could find plenty of material about you online, but what about JJ? I only know that he picked a great partner, barbecues a steak to perfection, and his handshake reveals inner strength. I admire people like that."

Jo nodded and grinned. "Can you get Tommy to permit us to work in parallel? I told him off at the hospital, and he may still be mad."

"I guess it's good that he asked me to help."

She felt the dread lift and smiled for the first time since Tommy arrived that morning. She opened the door and jumped down. "Thanks for the ride," she said.

"No problem. I'll speak with the chief either tonight or in the morning. I'll update you when I have something. If you need anything, give me a call."

Jo waved goodbye.

Jo wandered into their home, turning on lights here and there. Everything felt strange. She ran her hand over the top of the couch, touched chairs, checked the flowers for water, and then sat on a stool in the kitchen. She grabbed an orange from the fruit bowl and peeled it, running a thumbnail under the thick skin. Tears threatened to overrun her. She fisted the countertop and lamented, "JJ, what happened to our home? This is just a building without you." Her breathing grew ragged, but she fiercely cried, "I'm going to fix this problem, then I'm bringing you back home, wherever you decide we should be. I swear it!"

Jo pulled out her cell and followed the protocol to connect to Brayson.

He answered, "Hi, Jo. Did you make it home without any issues?"

"I did. Sorry to call you so late. Brandon Turner said he would help me. Tommy knows him. I didn't share anything about you, but I can give you any information I get."

"As long as you update me regularly, I'll work from Luxembourg. I got JJ's cell information and am decrypting it. I'll let you know tomorrow what I find." Following a long silence, Brayson said, "Jo, I've sparred in the gym with JJ for several years. In a fair fight, he's unstoppable."

Jo countered, "I've seen him in an unfair fight, and he still won. Share what you uncover. Mr. Turner is trying to set us up to visit the crime scene. I'll let you know what we find."

"Let's touch base in the morning."

Not Buying, Just Looking

Jo, ready to take on the world after some natural sleep, accepted Brayson's call while holding a fresh cup of juice.

"Morning, Jo. Don't be surprised when you read the local paper today. One man dead and one hospitalized in Magnolia Bluff is front-page news. Police are gathering evidence with multiple leads. Tommy must have the reporter on the hook because neither the realtor nor JJ is mentioned by name."

"Oh, dear. Now what?"

"I'll keep an eye on the news sources. If you feel threatened, you must let me know."

She wound a thick strand of hair around her finger while doubling her resolve. "I will, I promise. I want to help prove that JJ is innocent. Were you able to discover anything on our house computer?"

Brayson signed. "The good news is I got into your email family account, and it's full of SPAM."

Jo laughed, thinking of her experience with that digital plague. "I'm not technical, as you know, but SPAM's a regular email feature. They offer everything from date night romance by the minute to wrinkle cream for your posterior. I don't understand…"

Brayson interrupted, "No, this is different. A known series of SPAM addresses was sending thousands of emails to your family email in Magnolia Bluff with just one message:

Jo almost spit out her latest sip but carefully swallowed as his words registered. "That was the blackmailer, Brayson," she slowly gasped, thinking of the pressure he was facing.

Brayson grumbled, "Damn clever of him to anonymize his messaging with a SPAM engine to get JJ to react immediately. JJ would know there would be no way to respond or, more importantly, track the message back to a source. Even in a town the size of Magnolia Bluff, the time to get to that grocery store left no room for tracking, only enough time to generate the document access to the wallet. He probably funded it on the way, planning to let me know later."

Her phone vibrated, alerting her to another inbound call. She spotted Brandon's name in the window. "Brayson, let me know if anything else turns up. Brandon's on the other line."

One press on her screen later, she said, "Hi, Brandon. Did Tommy approve of us going to the house and looking, or is he still ticked at me?"

Brandon chuckled. "He wasn't delighted with the idea of civilians wandering over his crime scene, so much so that he couldn't wait to see us again at the scene in twelve minutes. I am almost to your gate."

"Did you happen to get a copy of the morning paper?"

"I found it on my driveway. It's pretty basic. The police are following leads and awaiting autopsy reports. JJ's name and condition weren't disclosed."

Jo grinned as she walked toward the bedroom to change into lightweight slacks, a tee shirt, and tennis shoes. She pressed the remote to open the front gate. "No problem. I'll be outside. I wouldn't want the shine from Tommy's mood to be dampened." She hung up and called Brayson back.

"Yes, ma'am," he said. "Good news?"

"We're heading to the crime scene."

"Call me later."

Jo disconnected the call, danced through the house like a ballerina, secured the alarm, and hurried outside. Tightening her hair into a single braid, she heard a car coming up the driveway. Butterflies gathered in her stomach as she set her jaw with determination.

Minutes later, Brandon pulled to the curb on Hickory Street and parked. He and Jo saw Reece Sovern talking with Tommy on the front lawn. Both men nodded as they approached.

Tommy was all business, saying, "Reece, go over it again so they can hear what we have so far in the case."

Reece rolled his unlit cigar to one side of his mouth, then straightened his stance. "No conventional weapon was used on the deceased. Someone knew exactly how to work a person over to get them to talk but not kill them. I was thinking of a baseball bat, but the coroner said no, as the impact areas are too small. He suggested the assailant used worn nunchaku sticks made of oak and probably chained together. Two splinters of oak were embedded in the victim's arm, where heavy bruising occurred. That type of device doubles as an impact club and can also be used to choke a person. The impact wounds covered most areas of his body. The neck area had an antemortem imprint of a metal chain consistent with the weapon's design. Jake sent a photo of the bruising to his contacts to try to identify the manufacturer."

Brandon added, "A nunchaku is most widely used in Southern Chinese kung fu, Okinawan Kob udo, and karate. It is intended to be used as a training weapon but is quite effective at targeting pain to parts of the body in agonizing bursts."

Tommy insisted, "Reece, I'm hungry. I missed breakfast. Go grab some donuts and coffee before we discuss our next steps." Tommy shoved a twenty into his hand and clarified, "Get me an assortment that includes chocolate covered with the little sprinkles. I want their jumbo double latte expresso infused with ginger and dandelion extract. I want room for cream, not milk, to be added. Get yourself some coffee, too."

Reece whined, "That place will be crowded at this time of day."

Brandon almost smiled as he saw the man open his mouth in protest. Tommy's glare forced him to think twice. Reece rolled his unlit cigar around his mouth several times before heading to his vehicle and getting in, punctuating his anger by slamming the door.

Once he was out of sight, Tommy handed each of them a pair of latex gloves and gruffly said, "Tell no one I did this. I never let you cross another crime scene tape. You were never here. Let's go before Reece returns."

CHAPTER 15

A Niche Business

Tommy took the lead under the yellow crime scene tape, unlocked the door, and pushed it open. One step into the entry hall, he froze. With his left arm, he blocked Jo and Brandon from entry. "Wait, I smell gas."

Brandon immediately asked, "Is the back door unlocked?"

Tommy shoved the key into his hand. Brandon bolted to the rear of the house. Moments later, he hollered, "Open!"

Tommy rushed to push up the first set of windows. "Jo, you can help open the windows in this area while I proceed." He shouted, "Brandon, let's find the leak. I'll check the garage and utility area. You can get the main rooms and hallway," Tommy stated.

"Got it," Brandon yelled. "It's the water heater line at the end of the hallway."

Tommy spotted Brandon's image in the mirror as he returned to the main room. "Tommy, the pilot light was out. It wasn't an accident. There's no natural air movement in that closet. I made sure with a few cranks the valve shut it off."

Tommy stood with them in the multipurpose area. He pointed out the chalk lines. "The one closest to us was where Rawley landed. The back one was where JJ was found. Step over those areas and avoid disturbing the lines. If you pick up anything, put it back in the same place. We've already dusted for prints and are awaiting the results."

Brandon coughed out the remainder of the gas residue. "Tommy, did the gas leak get missed yesterday, or is this something else?"

Tommy stared straight ahead as if replaying events from the prior day. Coming back to the present, he blinked. "When we arrived, both doors were open like now. There was no odor when I came in. Likely, if the gas leaked, it dissipated because of the airflow. Closing the house up allowed the gas to accumulate."

Brandon picked up a candle and matchbook from the fireplace's hearth and added them to the evidence bag Tommy provided. "Even though this might not seem out of place at the fireplace, maybe someone wanted to force an explosion to destroy all the evidence."

"Possible. But the plan was interrupted by something. Maybe Joyce's entry," said Tommy, as he made a note on the pad he'd extracted from his pocket.

"I bet the flue is shut like ours to avoid wasting air conditioning up the chimney," Jo added.

Brandon opened the screen and looked into the inky black area. "You're right, Jo. Not open."

Tommy added, "Good call, Jo."

"One or more persons blew out the pilot after dealing with both men. Joyce stumbled into the end of the crime, wigged out, and turned to leave," suggested Jo.

Brandon nodded. "That's a good theory. That would mean the perpetrators escaped, leaving the door open. The gas vented."

Tommy nodded and pursed his lips. "Jo, I had reservations about you being in here, but your thoughts make sense."

Tommy caught Brandon giving Jo a wink.

"Thankfully, it didn't get sparked. Bag up the candle and matches; you never know what the lab guys might find."

Brandon studied the scene and commented, "You have two people identified as being here, but I think there is a good chance one or more people were involved. We need to capture any missed evidence."

Jo looked between the two men. "Let's use our fresh eyes to find anything else that might have been missed."

Jo navigated around the chalk lines as they fanned out. She was drawn to the table crowded with papers and blank spaces near where the chair faced the desk. She mentally compared the space with where JJ worked. Messier, yet similar. She saw a mouse pad, a black mouse, scratchpads, and a lamp with sloppy piles tagged with numbered Post-it notes and printed sheets with photos. Jo noticed something that struck her as odd. She retrieved a pen from the holder with her gloved hand and called, "Hey, look at this." She used the pen to lift a power cable from the floor on the right side. "I think this is a computer power."

Brandon joined her, looking at the tabletop. "It's unlikely Rawley worked here without a laptop. Tommy, did your team confiscate a computer?"

Tommy walked next to them. "We checked the whole house. We found no computers but spotted a mobile phone power cable by the bedstand."

"Perhaps the others who were going to set a fire took it after immobilizing JJ and Rawley," Jo suggested.

Brandon grinned at her. He spotted a printer at the front of the desk. The light indicated it had power. "The printer's on. Someone once told me you can reprint documents if the printer's memory hasn't been cleared. I wonder if this one has that capability." He read the small instruction screen and pressed one button, then another. The device came to life and spit out page after page.

Tommy grabbed and read the last printed document. "Looks like your blackmail letter was generated here, Jo."

Brandon reviewed the other sheets and remarked, "Looks like your victim was a career blackmailer. These are other examples of his handiwork. I recognize two of the names as renowned politicians." He handed one of the letters to Tommy. "I thought I heard this one was in Fredericksburg, but he canceled an appearance at a book signing event due to last-minute family issues."

"Yes, it was quite the PR nightmare, though he promised to sign and ship his book for free to anyone who complained." Tommy chuckled. "The amount of recent book releases by politicians is staggering."

Brandon handed a page to Jo. She read it and shook her head. "I don't recognize Vladimir Sokolov as anyone famous or in the news. It appears to be the same type of demand for money." She gave it to Tommy.

"I agree, but I can do some research back at the office to see if his name comes up on any reports. The name looks Russian to me, so I can circulate it more widely, but we'll have to wait for a response. I've seen these things take weeks."

Jo snapped pictures of each of the letters with her cell phone. "This appears to be incriminating evidence. Anyone of these people could have felt the need to get even with Mr. Rawley. I know JJ didn't kill anyone." She jutted out her chin. "I want to help you find who did."

CHAPTER 16

Shopping for Answers

The three looked around the main room, realizing the donuts and coffee would arrive soon. The silence was interrupted by Tommy's ringtone. "Time to leave. We'll talk outside, and you can listen in on this." He swiped to answer and put it on speaker. Jo and Brandon preceded him into the front yard.

"Hey, Jake, whatcha got?"

"Tommy, thanks for having the hospital send me the pictures and measurements of the wounds on the other victim. You were right. The shapes, sizes, and bruising are identical. I believe a nunchaku weapon was used, but I don't yet have a specific brand. These are common in advanced Asian martial arts. I've sent some photos to colleagues to see if anyone recognizes the pattern of the marks. I can preliminarily conclude on this aspect that the victims were bludgeoned with the same device and likely by the same person due to the consistency and depth of the bruising. The man on my table was hit all over his body with varying force, as indicated by the marks. Even without having the exact weapon, each of them hurt. Based on the distance between some of the broken blood vessels under the surface, many strikes appear to have been delivered in rapid succession. The hospital staff provided me with a total count and photos. Patient Rodreguiz was struck heaviest in the torso front and side, with four notable marks on his head and neck area. He's lucky to be breathing."

Tommy looked to see Jo turn a pasty white and close her eyes. He inclined his head to Brandon to get her gloves and shoe covers, then headed slowly toward his cruiser.

Brandon collected the disposable coverings, handed them to Tommy, and patted Jo's shoulder. She responded with a resigned smile, leaning against the vehicle.

"Jake, what comes to mind if you had to characterize the order of the marks?" Tommy asked as he stuffed his coverings into the trash bag and saved the printed pages into an evidence bag, marking them with dates and times.

"My immediate impression was pain inflicted from the shins up. The first victim was likely sitting. An interrogation came to mind as the blows seemed to cause more pronounced marks with darker bruises."

"Any idea how long the beating for Rawley might have lasted?"

"Based on what I have seen, it would appear close to an hour. Broken blood vessels from blows, not cuts, cause various sizes, forms, and colors to head toward the skin's surface."

Tommy nodded. "After all the information was extracted, would it make sense that the end justified the means?"

"Could be. A methodical beating, I would suspect, was not the first delivered by the culprit." Jake clucked his tongue. "If I find anything further, I'll let you know."

Tommy disconnected the call and glanced at his watch. "You two must scoot before Reece and his tobacco pacifier return."

"Thanks for letting us take a look around," said Brandon.

"Jo, that was rough to hear," said Tommy. "Are you okay?"

Jo straightened her shoulders. "I'm good, Tommy, just more determined than ever to help you locate the person or persons who hurt my husband. I want them behind bars. I need to check on JJ with the hospital staff and see if I can visit later."

Brandon added, "You're farther along and have some leads to follow."

Tommy raised an eye. "You both found some overlooked items, so thank you."

"I'm sorry I shouted at you, Tommy," admitted Jo. "JJ and I believe you are our friend."

Tommy locked eyes with Jo, but he only nodded in silent agreement.

Jo got into the car and tugged on her seatbelt. "Brandon, can we swing by the Food Guys grocery store for a minute?"

"Do you need to shop before I take you home? I don't mind taking you." Brandon eyed her carefully as he pulled the car onto the street. "Or did you learn something from your home computer you didn't want to share with Tommy?"

Jo blew out a breath, glad for Brandon's comment. "Yes, I found something in our family email account before you called to say you were picking me up. It was filled with SPAM messages, all saying the same thing. *Go to Food Guys grocery store for instructions on how to deliver the payment.*"

Brandon's eyes widened as he focused on the traffic. "JJ planned to pay the blackmailer without any further investigation by authorities? Pardon me for asking, but do you folks keep a hundred grand lying around the house for impulse purchases or ransom demands?"

Jo twisted her fingers and laughed. "No, we don't keep that kind of cash around. The original note from the blackmailer requested cryptocurrency. JJ is fluent in handling crypto and could easily access that much in short order for bargaining."

"In my experience," Brandon mused, "this is where the crooks do the bouncing game with the victim to separate them from the ransom and not get tracked. All right, let's investigate the store. From what I've seen, you demonstrate good intuition." He inclined his head. "Happy to be of service, but you might have mentioned it to Tommy."

CHAPTER 17

Part Truth

Brandon stopped the vehicle at the far side of the Food Guys parking lot so they could observe the traffic flow. Saturday morning traffic would have been lighter than today's. Their eyes roved the area from the vehicle windows for several minutes before either spoke.

"Jo, how do you know JJ came here?"

"I don't, but I thought it was a possibility. Let me show you." Jo scrolled the screen of her phone until she found the photo Brayson had sent. "I snapped the email account of one of the items. They were so weird, all from different email addresses, meaning it would be unlikely JJ could have identified the sender with any confidence. This one was from *87hmars@201g.2zzz. eu*. JJ has told me before that if you hover over the address and it switches to something else, it's SPAM." She turned toward him and added, "He said if we received any instructions, he could give it to Tommy. We agreed to this when the letter was discovered at the house." She pointed to the top edge of the photo. "The email stated a time limit, so he wouldn't have had time to call Tommy and drive safely. I think he was going to follow the directions and then call."

Brandon's brow furrowed as he squinted his eyes while look-ing at her phone, knowing something wasn't right. He pinched the screen to resize different areas and then scanned the parking lot. "This is a crisp photo you captured off a PC screen?"

She twisted her fingers but said nothing, nor did she look in his direction.

Brandon scanned the photo, then turned it toward her, and, using his finger, he continued. "The reflection on this parked car at the side looks like your rental car. Note that it looks like a sign. This would make this image more likely from a cell phone rather than one sent to an email early in the morning. That suggests it came from JJ's cell phone, which is in police custody." He caught her eye, and quietly stated, "How could you have a photo extracted from an impounded cell phone?"

Jo squirmed in her seat and looked at her hands. He figured her brain was running around in that lovely head, searching for how to fix her story. He waited.

She looked up with guilty tears forming in her eyes.

He sighed. "It's okay, just breathe. I think JJ works with folks in the intelligence community, which is why I couldn't find any background on him. Someone sent this to you after getting it remotely from JJ's phone to provide details to let you help get to the bottom of this mess."

She closed her eyes and almost imperceptibly nodded.

"That's why you didn't tell Tommy about the SPAM emails earlier. We'll need to share this with him at some point. I'm willing to hold it back for now. His team will find it if they break into the phone unless it's already been removed." Taking her chin gently with a single finger, he made sure she looked at him. "I'm glad we're getting help, but I would appreciate it if you would not concoct any stories about anything you bring to our investigation. I'm on your side. I will help you get to the truth."

"Okay," she whispered. "I'm sorry, Brandon. JJ is good at his job. He works with great people who stay behind the scenes. I promised to inform them if they didn't come to Magnolia Bluff and ruin any chance of our remaining here with friends. They are trying to protect me and JJ."

He patted her hand, convinced they had an honest understanding. "I understand and respect that you're holding confidences. I won't press you, but I will follow the leads. I also think you have great observation skills. Let me see that image again. I want to park my truck in the same position to see if we spot any clues."

He relocated the truck, grateful for the lull in shoppers. They got out to survey the parking lot.

"Can you read the words on the sign, please?" Brandon requested.

Jo used her thumb to enlarge the sign in the photo and grinned.

> **Blessed are the famous who donate generously for the poor.**
> — Rodreguiz Psalm

Brandon smirked. "The blackmailer put up a sign with religious connotations no one would think twice about except JJ." He pointed to the edge of the parking lot. "There, Jo, see the collection container. I bet it's for charity. JJ was directed there to make a deposit."

Jo's face reflected confusion. "I don't understand."

Brandon quietly explained. "Bouncing the target here and there is all part of the exercise to extract the ransom and get away unseen. Let's inspect the box."

They walked over to the cracked asphalt to the worn container, which was decorated with rude graffiti in places. Brandon noticed the furniture piled in front of the twenty-footer, with its peeling paint, wouldn't fit in the pull-down door. He pulled the chain and looked inside the metal slide. The sunlight exposed an empty interior. "No clothing in here." They slowly walked around the storage box, seeing the ravages of time and weather.

Jo exclaimed, "Look, the back door has been forced open."

"Be careful," Brandon cautioned. "There may be fingerprints Tommy could get for the investigation."

"How can we ask Tommy to dust for fingerprints without saying why we were here?"

Brandon chuckled. "You're getting good at this detective stuff. How about we show him the cast-off sign sitting over there?" He pointed. "The rest of the SPAM story is still good, telling JJ where to go. Tommy may want to see the email account."

Jo smiled. "You want to call him, or shall I?"

CHAPTER 18

The Second Mouse gets the Cheese

The phone's familiar Beethoven's Overture ring pulled Jo from a terrifying dream back into reality. She pressed the button, squinting toward the blinds, and noticed the blush of sunrise peeking through the sides. "Hi, Brayson," she yawned. "Did you get to review the photos?" she yawned again. "I sent?"

She heard a mimic yawn and chuckle.

Chuckling slightly, he replied, "Please stop, now you've got me yawning. Yep, it didn't take long to get two of the backstories. Hoo-boy. Career politicians are like barnacles on a whale who believe public funds are easier pickings than shoplifting at a department store. The Vladimir character took longer to locate and cross-reference the information. At this juncture, he's the only Russian gangster in his country forced to leave. It's funny, too, as he was a founding member of a notorious money laundering, narcotics wholesaling, weapons brokering, and human trafficking operation. He vanished when five government agencies simultaneously attacked the operation's darknet website and put it out of commission. If one wanted a poster child for cyber-scum, his name would top the list with a tag line—he kicks dogs, too."

Jo straightened in bed, pulled up the luxurious bamboo sheets, and leaned against the headboard with her hand resting on JJ's pillow. "Seriously, the jerk who was trying to blackmail us stupidly chose to blackmail a Russian cyber thug? That's rich."

"Everything I've uncovered so far suggests he pulled up stakes in Russia when authorities detained his coworkers as they attempted to sneak over the border. Somehow, Vladimir vanished unscathed but was suspected of crossing into the United States with a new identity. I found a facial recognition match to a man posing as an executive foreign movie producer in California last year, Vlad Kolov. The trail ended after Vlad skipped with several million dollars he'd collected to bring a blockbuster story to the silver screen. A dozen investors were fleeced and filed charges. That movie will never get produced."

Jo laughed and then parroted back the story to make sure she had it straight to relate to Brandon. "Did you find any information on Mr. Rawley that might prove useful?"

"There's not much on the man," Brayson related, "out of his moving around doing part-time programming through a temp agency. He collects a routine paycheck auto-deposited into a checking account in New York. Some of his efforts suggest he supported illegal and unlawful operations. Rawley could have cross-paths during his not-so-legal side jobs. It's hard to verify those interactions, but I'm still digging. I did find evidence of potential victims who refused his ransom demands. Rawley's information was published for the world to see, ruining a couple of careers."

Jo mused, "Do you think Vladimir could have fought back?"

"It's possible, but even the politicians have money and power to make problems disappear or to get even."

"The coroner told Tommy the beating marks on both individuals were the same size, but he ruled out a baseball bat. No guns or shell casings were found. He believes nunchaku was used as a weapon. The coroner suggested that the assailant was probing for information and that the beating was the motivator."

"Jo," Brayson admitted, "I'll keep digging, but any information you can share will make it easier to find the pieces to this puzzle until JJ wakes up. Doctor Brewer has received JJ's medical records and will have a video conference with his doctor in charge later today. His condition is stable but unchanged."

Jo was overcome with loneliness and sniffled. "I'll try to get a few minutes with him later today. Hopefully, the sound of my voice will help bring him back to me."

"He'll know you're there, Jo. Don't despair. Call me anytime."

"Thank you, Brayson." Jo grabbed a tissue from the nightstand, dabbed her eyes, and blew her nose.

"I'm going to poke around on JJ's laptop remotely. Make certain the printer is on in case I find anything I want you to have in hand."

"I'll send his latest login and password in case it gets rebooted," Jo added.

"Thanks, Jo. We'll figure this out. You're doing a great job."

CHAPTER 19

What are the Odds?

Brandon arrived with Max early at Joyce's for breakfast. He'd donned jeans, a light blue polo shirt, and tennis shoes, planning to take Jo around and check out more leads. Jason kept Joyce laughing, recanting the ball team's group text about the upcoming away game, so her spirits were high as she served the meal. After eating the delicious food, Jason completed kitchen duty quickly, kissed his mom goodbye, and left. Brandon was about to leave when she held up a finger and hurriedly scribbled on the ever-present pad. *The memories remain sketchy, but I'm sleeping better. Jason loves driving himself.*

He read it and grinned. "Glad you're resting. How's your voice?"

She opened her mouth, and a squeak sounded, "Nah," followed by a crooked smile and a head shake. She added to the pad. *I swear it sounded better in the shower this morning. You look nice; is a busy day planned?*

Brandon couldn't resist a giggle. "That's good, honey. You haven't lost your sense of humor." He gave her a quick hug. "Do you feel like trying to write about the images floating in your mind? Maybe you'll create a jigsaw puzzle we can put together with time. Just a thought."

She nodded with a smile.

"I need to pick up Jo this morning. JJ is stable. The doctor will let her visit for a few minutes. I'll update you later on all the news. Thank you for watching my dog today."

She leaned into him for a hug, then stood on tiptoes for a kiss. She wiggled her fingers as he left.

Brandon entered the code to the gate Jo provided, pulled near the barn, and parked. As he got out, he spotted her in a bright shirt and khaki shorts watering the flowers. She waved him toward the house after she turned the spigot off.

"Morning, Jo."

"Hey, Brandon, do you want coffee before we leave?" she offered with a practiced smile.

"Sure," he replied, raising an eyebrow when he caught the earnest look in her eyes. "We can catch up."

Grinning at the comment, she led the way through the side door into the kitchen. He sat at the table, noticing the fresh-cut flowers. "From your garden?"

She set down a fresh cup in front of him. "Yes. They are starting to do well, but they love the morning watering, so it's become a ritual." Returning with her cup and a plate of small plain croissants, she sat. "The blend is American style; I know you prefer it."

"Thank you. What's up?" he asked, snagging one of the snacks.

She laughed. "JJ says I'm pretty poor at keeping secrets at times. I received a call from my remote support about the black-mail letter pictures I took yesterday. While watering the plants, I realized I must tell you everything I know because I'm uncertain what I should share with Tommy versus what he should discover on his own."

Brandon sipped his coffee as a wave of relief rushed through his mind. "Good to hear. I'm on your side. Let's discuss what you heard, then I'll help you sort it out. I do believe Tommy is also on your side."

"I think so, too, but he's in a tough spot." Jo carefully repeated everything Brayson had told her, itemized with good details. Arching his eyebrows, Brandon was stunned by the amount of information she'd learned.

He swallowed his third roll. "Nicely done, Jo. We have a list of possible suspects who were highly motivated to find and end the blackmailing. It sounds like Vladimir is the front-runner, but we have unanswered questions regarding his whereabouts. The others have a lot of press coverage when they sneeze, so they're easier to find. They also have different resources to call upon," She air quoted with her fingers, "to 'fix' problems."

Jo tilted her head, appearing confused. "Who in their right mind would attempt to blackmail these famous, notorious people, expecting no retribution?"

Brandon blinked, and quietly said, "Rawley didn't get away with it. We, including Tommy, are confident he was a career blackmailer. We don't know who showed him his errors in such a final manner. You only need to watch the news to know some career politicians can be quite persuasive when confronted with their indiscretions. There's something about being elected, then having everyone learn your dastardly deed, that makes some people fight for the power they think they deserve."

"You don't think Vladimir is a viable suspect?" Jo asked.

"Rawley was a two-bit petty blackmailer who unearthed some dirt on renowned politicians. Vladimir's a full-time crook who can buy new identities and is wanted on several continents. What are the odds of this bozo finding Vladimir, the cyber ghost, then threatening him with exposure unless he gets some serious coin?"

Jo shrugged her shoulders and then tapped her chin with a manicured nail. "Whoever reasoned with Rawley would have had to come to town and research extensively to find him. He recently rented that house. JJ did his homework, knew where to look, and got there ahead of the killer. When you come to a small town looking for a certain someone, wouldn't you spend a couple of days surveying the landscape? Wouldn't you need a place to stay and perhaps ask discreet questions of folks who know everybody?"

Brandon smiled and commented with a nod toward her deductive skills. "You mean like staying at the Flower Bed and Breakfast and chatting with the owner and the regulars who take a meal there. Small towns are gossip centers. There's also the bar we could check too."

Jo grinned and exclaimed, "If we hurry, we might get brunch."

CHAPTER 20

Greetings, Friend

Brandon and Jo inhaled the delicious aromas of omelets, French toast, pancakes, and coffee as they strolled into the Flower B&B dining area. Brandon leaned and whispered, "Heck, I already had breakfast with Joyce and ate your flaky rolls, but this makes me hungry again."

"Lily knows how to cook. Everything tastes even better than it smells. I like her fresh berries."

Lily was collecting payment from the last of the breakfast crowd at the register. "Nice to talk to you this morning, Caroline. Have a quiet day at the library."

"Thanks, Lily," said Caroline. "I'll look for that book you wanted." She turned and spotted Jo. "Hey, Jo, I enjoyed your party. Brandon, you must be here picking up breakfast for Joyce. I'd love to talk, but I gotta go. Lily, thanks for staying open a little later."

Frowning at Lily after waving goodbye to Caroline, Jo huffed, "We're too late for even brunch?"

Lily laughed. "You, too late for food here? It never happens. Get your fanny into the seat of the clean table by the window and let me know what you have a hankering to eat. I'll feed the ex-detective, too, for a smile and a hug."

Lily received a friendly embrace and waved her hands toward the open table. After they sat, Lily scurried around for cups, served coffee and juice, and then sat again. With a somber expression and a pat on Jo's hand, she asked, "I saw the paper this morning. I noticed JJ's name wasn't there. Tommy said he was in the hospital when he stopped in last evening for dinner and asked me not to tell anyone. Has there been any change in his condition?"

"He's stable at this point. I can see him for a few minutes later today. I'll let you know when I get updates. Plus, I'll meet with his doctors to hear their treatment plans."

Lily turned toward Brandon. "Can Joyce hustle people again with her realtor speak?"

Brandon wanted to remain upbeat. "It is a perfect storm for me. Joyce can't speak, and I, like Jason, don't realize the necessary chores without her notes. Jason pushes the limits by announcing he's leaving to see his friends as he walks out the door. She can't write loud enough to demand he *get back here and do the dishes*. It could be he's goading her into getting mad enough to speak."

Lily swatted his arm and chortled. "Jason would never do that. However, your storytelling is improving. There's always a silver lining, huh? Let's get some grub for you both; then we can gab and swap lies." She rubbed her hands together. "I can't wait."

They chuckled.

Lily jumped up, collected the remaining dishes on the tables, and wiped them with a practiced hand. "I wish Renata hadn't already slipped off to school. It won't take me long to fix some plates. Any special requests, all y'all?"

"I'm in for fruit," said Jo.

"I'm good with anything you have, Lily. It's always delicious."

"Leftovers are coming right up. It saves me from having to put them away. You make me proud to know you, son." Lily chuckled as she ferried the dishes to the kitchen.

Noise from the kitchen barely interrupted the pleasant dining room. Light glowed in from the windows, and the flowers' vibrant reds, blues, purples, yellows, and whites were visible.

Jo commented, "I hope my garden will become that abundant."

"I'm sure it will. It's off to a great start," said Brandon as he added coffee from the carafe Lily had left behind to his cup.

Lily shuttled out plates, silverware, napkins, and several platters of food to self-serve in the middle of the table.

She joined them with a cup of fresh coffee. "Well? Spill it."

Brandon looked around, making sure they were alone. "Lily, we have a working theory about the uh…crime that Tommy's working."

Lily frowned. "You mean the one where Mr. Rawley was killed. JJ didn't do it." She reached over and squeezed Jo's hand to convey support. "It's about time someone asked me if he was nosey. Even when I spoke to Tommy, he never asked if the man had stopped here to eat. Almost everyone who visits or lives in this town eats here at one time or another. I didn't much care for him, and I know you shouldn't speak ill of the departed, but he was kind of stinky and slovenly. I swear he wore the same jeans three days in a row. That man had no calluses on his hands, so he was no day laborer. He ordered two eggs sunny side up, a short stack of pancakes, and a side of grits. Not many folks like grits, especially not every day. Oh, and coffee—at least a pot. He asked about different people, usually the ones seated or leaving. He always requested the back corner table."

"What makes you think that's why we're here?" Jo asked.

Lily rolled her eyes. "Honey, small-town women have extra helpings of common sense. Both of you have dear ones affected, motivating you to find the truth. Jo, you've always been that way. Though I don't know you well, Brandon, with your background as a detective, I suspect it's in your nature." She paused to take a big sip of her coffee. Brandon noticed a twinkle in her eyes as she looked toward him. "Fact is, I like knowing everyone else's business. I don't have a shy bone in my body about asking. I can be compassionate, instructive, empathetic, flirtatious, and downright nosey when I meet people. That's why folks trust me and tell me more than they should. Who are you looking for?"

"We have information we haven't given to Tommy yet," Jo said. "We want your observation so we can confidently deliver good leads to him."

Lily rubbed her hands together, making Brandon chuckle. "Lily, we'd like your opinion kept confidential."

She looked at him with an easy smile, crossed her heart with her right hand, and raised a palm. "You can trust me."

Brandon stated, "Anything you can provide us about Mr. Rawley or his conversations with you or that you overheard could help. We'll sort it out. Any interesting or suspicious conversations in the last few months could be important."

Lily grinned. "I get it. I'll talk while you enjoy the food. Let me grab another pot of coffee for the table." She rushed to the kitchen and returned in seconds, sliding into her seat as smoothly as a runner gliding into home plate.

"Glad to see you helped yourself."

Brandon couldn't help but notice Lily scooting around, getting comfortable in the chair, and tilting her head. Her theatrics were well-practiced.

Lily cleared her throat. "I've had folks stay here and ask more questions than I can recant. Some offered answers, and some lied. One oily politician pretended to be canvassing for votes but based on his questions, was hunting for someone in particular. I swear that man couldn't pour urine out of a boot with instructions written on the heel."

Brandon chuckled, and Jo grinned.

"Another fellow came for breakfast," Lily continued. "Boy, he was different. He had a funny Russian accent but didn't mind being teased. We got along well. He even tried to teach me some

Russian. He and I got to cutting up. I made him laugh with my limited pigeon Russian. I said, let me prove I know some Russian, 'I'll greet you in your language.' I held up my hand and hailed him with *Fyodor Mikhailovich Dostoevsky.* I swear to you, his coffee almost flowed from his ears; he was laughing so hard."

Brandon closed his eyes and pinched his nose bridge, envisioning the conversation.

Jo giggled. "I thought *Fyodor Dostoevsky* was a writer, Lily. Am I wrong?"

Lily frowned, appearing devastated. "If I have to explain it to you, it's not funny anymore." She sniffled into a tissue pulled from her pocket. "Of course he is. I was playing the country bumkin for this guy. If people think you're sharp as a bowling ball, they hand out willy-nilly. He asked questions about internet service, new residents, and other odd questions that told me he was on a hunting expedition. He might be someone worth speaking to. He returned one other time for dinner. I was too busy to visit, and Renata served all the tables. I'm not sure if he spoke to any of the other diners."

Brandon asked, "Can you describe him?"

"He seemed pleasant, about your size, maybe a little heavier. Dark hair with waves and highlights of grey, a bit on the longish side. His beard was trimmed, he had no jewelry, good white teeth when he smiled or laughed, and wore an intoxicating scent of musk. His eyes were the most striking feature—almost black. He was friendly, but I sensed an undercurrent of anger swirling behind his smile. Oh, his hands were beefy. I only noticed because he gave me his orange juice when we spoke and promised we would have vodka and toast sometime. Does that help?"

Brandon nodded. "It does. You have impressive recall, Lily."

CHAPTER 21

The Senator Will See You

Heat radiated in the morning air at quarter to eight when Tommy unlocked the police station doors. He marched in with his usual tall coffee, hoping for quiet time. Sitting in his worn chair, he planned to jot notes to help structure the day between intermittent sips of coffee. His cell phone twinned to the office simultaneously blared, breaking silence and foreboding a poor day ahead. He closed his eyes, spotting the recognized caller identification.

"Chief Tommy Jager. How can I help you?"

"Senator David here. Tommy, good morning."

The chief sipped his coffee, hearing the paternal vote-for-me voice from a man he'd never help get elected. Tommy impatiently replied, "What can I do for you?"

"I'm close to your office. I want to get up to speed on your murder investigation. Being a local representative, I must be read in."

Tommy raised his eyes to survey the street through the window and spotted the limo parked in front. He rolled his eyes, clucked his tongue, and sarcastically asked, "Did you bring donuts?"

"No, but I can send my driver to retrieve…"

Determined to make the politician wait, Tommy added some items to his list, then scratched out one.

"Are you still there, Chief?"

"Never mind about the donuts. I've got lots on my plate today." He shook his head, refusing a promise to meet the request. "Come on in. Let's get your issue cleared up as soon as possible."

"On my way."

Minutes later, the door opened and closed. Tommy watched Senator David lumber toward his office, wearing his expensive tailored jacket—too tight at the belly, silk tie, and enviable Stetson. The man's hair was trimmed like his barber was in the limo, which wouldn't surprise Tommy if that was the case. He reached out to shake hands as he approached the worn oak desk, which Tommy ignored.

"Take a seat, senator."

"Harumph. I can influence with the powers that be, Chief. Common courtesy and displaying a willingness to play ball wouldn't hurt. Where are you at in your investigation?"

"It's funny, senator. I was about to call your office to ask you to see me about that very subject. But here you are. I find myself wondering why you'd be here after the local paper published a story of one man being killed and another in the hospital with police investigating."

"Murders are big news even in small towns like Magnolia Bluff."

Tommy chuckled and looked pointedly at the man. "They are important to our community, but this is the first one you've stuck your nose into. We've had several in Magnolia Bluff, sir."

The man shifted in the hard chair. "I've been campaigning around this area and felt it my civic duty to be informed. How did the man die?"

"As the article in the paper said, Mr. Rawley had recently rented a house. He worked from home in an undisclosed business. What isn't in the paper is that his neck was broken after he was beaten. I asked for that part to be left out for the time being. The other part that was not shared with the press was the blackmail letters recovered. We're investigating those victims of what appears to be Mr. Rawley's livelihood."

Senator David's tanned face drained of color and sweat popped on his forehead. He mopped his brow with his designer pocket square, breathed, and demanded, "Was one of those letters mine? I want it destroyed before anyone else sees it—my wife, for one, and my campaign manager, for another. I can't have slanderous propaganda floating around during my re-election for state senator campaign."

Tommy realized he had a leak, or this man knew far too much as an innocent victim. "I didn't share the information on the potential victims of Mr. Rawley. And I don't care that you are a—" he added air quotes— 'powerful man.' Tampering with evidence is against the law, especially in an ongoing murder investigation. How did you know I might have a blackmail letter with your name on it? I know you're not stupid enough to think you wouldn't be a suspect, especially huffing and puffing your way into my office. Since you're here, I will ask you some questions and take your statement of where you were at the time of Mr. Rawley's death."

Terror crossed the pompous man's face. He stuttered, "Perhaps we got off on the wrong foot this morning, Chief Jager. You are an exemplary officer of the law. I'm guessing that, like other offices upholding justice, you lack funding. I am happy to put in a good word for additional city funding at the next state session."

Ignoring the thinly disguised bribe, Tommy gruffly demanded, "I need to know where you were on Sunday and Monday of this week hour by hour. I need witnesses to corroborate your whereabouts."

The pitiful man swallowed hard, making Tommy wish he could take and share that photo with voters.

"My staff has my schedule for each day clearly and precisely accounted for, so I can keep my campaign commitments. You can rest assured that…"

Tommy continued his line of questioning. "Somewhat odd that your campaign trail for re-election has you canvassing Magnolia Bluff for three full days that I know of. How long have you been in town? Should we bring in your aid to help answer…"

Senator David's nostrils flared as he tried to deflect the conversation. "I think we're done here, Chief. Don't hesitate to contact my office for an appointment if you need more information."

Tommy smirked. "I want you to stay in town for more questioning. We'll need to talk again tomorrow, at this same time, with your appointment schedule for review. Don't forget the donuts."

The senator rose and stormed out.

CHAPTER 22

A Little Help from Friends

Late in the afternoon, Jo arrived at the security desk in the ICU. The wide-screen monitors showed the patients' last names and colors, reflecting various devices that echoed current status signals for easy review by medical staff. The duty nurse confirmed Jo's identity and handed her a garb to cover her clothes. The nurse took Jo to JJ's room, where she nodded to the officer on duty. Jo's stomach lurched at the sight of the extra tubes connected to him, reminding her of a battered voodoo doll.

"Mrs. Rodreguiz, you'll have about fifteen minutes until the doctor arrives. You can touch him. All the sensors are secure. I know it looks frightening, but it allows us to monitor him effectively."

"Thank you, ma'am," said Jo. She approached the side of the bed and took JJ's hand as the nurse closed the door. Jo's eyes misted up but didn't overflow.

After a few ragged breaths, she whispered, "Honey, I've been watering the flowers in the morning like we do in *São Paulo*. I try to do it before the sun clears the house because the August heat is unforgiving, according to Lily. I wish…" Jo sobbed as tears rolled down her face. His skin felt lukewarm, unlike the heat when he moved or held her. "JJ, please wake up. Come back to me. I want you with me. You are my rock, though I am trying to find answers."

The hushed conversation outside the door caused her to wipe her face. She used one of the tissues at the table by his side to blow her nose. She leaned in and kissed his cheek. "I love you so much."

A young blond-haired doctor strode up to her. "Mrs. Rodreguiz, I'm Doctor Sampson, the physician in charge of your husband at this juncture. There has been no significant change in his condition outside of his fever dissipating. I've witnessed many patients with comas. I know it's hard for families who feel helpless. Each patient in a coma is different. It would seem his body is working to recover as he has no swelling or other telltale signs of anything that requires surgery or more invasive treatment. He is receiving fluids with no problems. We are not seeing the movement yet under his eyelids, which would signal he is returning. Talking to coma patients has always been seen as beneficial. At this point, he needs rest to recover from the inside out. You may come in early in the morning before nine and return around half past eight in the evening for no more than thirty minutes for the next few days because he's in the ICU, not a private room. The nurse on duty may ask you to leave sooner if needed. We want his recovery almost as much as you do."

She lifted her head and implored, "You're saying there's no timeline. It could be days or weeks before he comes back to me. Is there anything else or another specialist I might engage to help you and your team?"

"Dr. Brewer and I spoke to his doctor in Luxembourg. He asked about several procedures that could be employed. Those advanced procedures are experimental and not available here. Moving him to another hospital in Dallas or Houston is ill-advised in his condition. His doctor agrees with the current treatment plan. I update him when I arrive on shift and when I leave. Of course, we will reach out if the situation changes. He promised to provide any resources we needed. I thanked him, but for now, he is stable." He cleared his throat. "I offered to let him use our robotic diagnostic appliance to observe over video, but after our discussion, he declined. I'm taking that as a vote of confidence in the care we are providing."

Jo felt reassured as she stroked JJ's arm. "The medical team is doing all it can, and the rest is up to you to fight for. I'll return in the morning and bring a book to read to you with the doctor's permission." She glanced at the doctor and grinned.

He nodded. "After all you two have done for this small town, I am glad we can help. Try to be patient. Call a half hour before you arrive tomorrow. The staff will make certain you get in."

CHAPTER 23

Long Day

Brandon took Jo by the store for groceries and then dropped her at home, promising he would arrive around eight the following morning. When he pulled into Joyce's driveway, he was lost in thought, sifting through Lily's comments. He entered the front door and called, "Hi, anybody home? It's me."

Max bounded out of the kitchen, Joyce right behind him. Brandon ruffled Max, half petting and half wrestling with him. "Were you a good boy today? Only good boys get treats."

Brandon smiled as Joyce approached, shaking her head and scribbling on the notepad. *He peed in the kitchen before I could get him outside.*

Brandon scolded, "Max, we've talked about this. You do your business outside, or it's the circus outsourcing job."

Brandon saw the angry frustration reflected on Joyce's face. Almost as a reflex to ease the tension, he glibly stated, "Maybe I could get you an air horn to get everyone's attention while you write out your orders."

Every mortal man who has ever aggravated a woman recognizes the look of a category-five storm about to rage. Joyce roared, "NOT FUNNY, BRANDON!"

Brandon rocked back on his heels, astonished at the sound of her voice.

Joyce clapped her hands over her mouth, then rushed to embrace him with all her pent-up emotions. After a frantic embrace, Brandon danced up and down, wildly swinging her around. "All right, honey. I want to hear you again."

Tears of joy streamed down her face as she repeated the words in a lower tone, with a raspy edge.

Delighted by this change, he asked, "And your disconnected memories? Are they back?"

Joyce's shoulders slumped, and she shook her head. "Still pieces, though I did start to describe the flashing pictures. It's almost like being somewhere with a strobe light…and mirrors. Odd."

Brandon pulled her into a hug. "One battle at a time. You can talk, which is awesome."

Joyce swallowed. "It's wonderful," her voice still gravelly.

Brandon mischievously grinned. "Does this mean Jason and I are off chore duty?"

Joyce frowned and squinched her eyes. "Nope. I'm milking this for a while longer."

Jo had no sooner put the groceries away when her phone beeped, indicating someone was at the gate. The app on her cellphone displayed Hank and Ann's truck. Pressing the admit key, she removed a few glasses and took them to the pergola, setting them on a table.

From the window, Jo noticed the truck had barely been parked when Ann bolted from the vehicle, closely followed by Hank. Hank's limp and the picnic basket he toted slowed him down. Ann barreled straight to the side door, nearly colliding with Jo, who emerged after turning smooth jazz to play through the speakers.

Ann jammed her fists on her hips as she admonished, "You're carrying the weight of the world on your shoulders with JJ in the hospital, but I have to hear about it from my kids and the gossip mill?"

Hank limped up and soothed, "Ann, honey, let's not dress her down on top of everything she's facing." He set the basket on the table and hugged Jo. "Girl, we're a little hurt you didn't reach out. We want to support you. We insist on helping until you get past this bad patch."

"Jo, in this part of the world," Ann said, "you call on friends and tell them when everything is going to hell in a handbasket. That way, we can help you swear at the evil turn of fate and rush over with fixings to fill you up. Based on your non-existent tummy, you haven't eaten nearly enough in a while. You and JJ mean as much to us as the two young girls you helped us adopt. Please, don't you dare suffer all this alone."

Hank's eyes were a bit misty as he nodded in agreement.

Jo, nearly unable to contain the pent-up emotions without tears, hugged her dear friends. "It was wrong of me not to let you know. I'm sorry. With everything spiraling down the drain of despair, I didn't feel it fair to burden you while we're keeping JJ's name out of the mainstream news."

Ann patted her arm. "Sweetie, we brought light finger foods like brisket, pinto beans, slaw, potato salad, and cobbler to ensure you keep up your strength."

Hank said, "I brought the perfect whiskey to help wash it down."

Jo smirked at their touching, neighborly gesture. "Please come in. I'll tell you what I can, but so much is under police investigation."

Ann unpacked, setting out the paper plates and serving containers.

Hank winked. "Jo, do you have some shot-size glasses for the whiskey? And a tumbler-size for me?"

Jo returned with the glasses and took a seat, noticing Hank's plate overflowing. He poured generous quantities into the glasses.

Jo chuckled, raising her glass, grateful for this wonderful surprise that filled her heart with joy. "Cheers. What have you heard from the gossipers, Ann?"

CHAPTER 24

Time to See the Man

Jo rolled over, reaching for her phone on the nightstand to silence the demanding sounds of the *Earthquake* symphony. It was so loud. In her mind, her perky greeting sounded garbled. "Gumbmorninishbabalouie."

Brayson chuckled. "Sorry, Jo. Did I wake you? I'll bet you can't wait to get rid of conversations with people eight-plus hours ahead of your time zone. Heck, I'm on my second pot of coffee."

Jo struggled into a sitting position, yawning to clear the sleep cobwebs. "I'm awake but not coherent." Standing, she pulled on her silk robe and looped the tie. "I know you're going to share new information. Talk while I stagger to the kitchen to get my first cup. If only you could have coffee magically appear before your call." She slipped into her slippers and made her way to the coffee. Setting her phone on the counter, she put it on speaker. "Go ahead, I'm a captive audience."

Brayson related, "Using your information, I did more digging. First, Rawley doesn't have large bank accounts, on or offshore. He was fired from his last job for spending half his days surfing the net. He subcontracts piecemeal programming. Second, Brandon's comment suggesting Rawley was an internet super sleuth and catching Vladimir when no government agency has to date stung, so I did more research on the people named in the letters you provided. I dug into Senator David. As far as I can tell, he's as squeaky clean as a week-old fish thrown into a septic tank. Phew, does this guy stink? One journalist said, '*Senator David is the best politician money can buy*.' Remarkably, he has time to campaign for re-election. He and his staff fully walked back the fallout from his indiscretions. If he isn't hustling some developer to get in on their money-making project, he's hushing up a sexual harassment charge leveled against him by some girl's father."

Jo wrinkled her nose. "He sounds like a piece of work." She added coffee to the bright orange cup and inhaled the scent of chocolate in the dark liquid.

"Yep. His aids are doing so much damage control that they can't keep an eye on him. But he keeps getting re-elected, so he's somehow resonating with voters."

"And the others?" Jo asked. "Do they have equally gross secrets worth blackmailing to conceal?"

Brayson chuckled. "Everyone has something to hide. However, the others seem to be practice accounts. The amounts asked for were paltry compared to the top three six-figure demands. He was practicing on them with false accusations to see how his business model might work. He went from cheesy people to world-class candidates rather quickly. Overreaching got him killed, however."

Jo nodded, thinking for a few sips. "Nice to know I'm in the top three, but in yucky company. We'll see Tommy this morning and disclose what we've found. Brandon is keeping my outreach with you to himself."

"Good, but Tommy's no fool. I poked around on JJ's machine and found the directory he created for the blackmailer. The USB drive he was to deliver to break free of this clown possibly had some extra goodies. Did JJ give you any hint of what he was concocting?"

"I told you he left early that morning, and I didn't speak with him. I assumed that he got the blackmail request and there was a time limit. Brandon said it was a bouncing technique to ensure criminals can get their money and dodge anyone tailing the target."

"Makes sense. I'll work on the materials I found in that directory to see if I can determine what he planned. Something might turn up. At least I know how he works."

Jo replied, "Thank you. I need to get ready to go. Talk later."

Jo was standing outside her house as Brandon drove up. Opening the door, she placed her shoulder strap purse on the floor and slid into the seat. "Good morning. How's Joyce doing? Any change?"

Brandon beamed, nodding like a kid who won a front-row seat at the first major league playoff game in October. "She was frustrated and yelled at me. We hop-danced around the kitchen. Her voice was still scratchy but ready to say goodbye to scribbling notes. Her memory is still in pieces, or snatches of images, she calls them. I estimate she's missing roughly three hours of memories. I suggested she draw the images or write about them."

"Perfect. I'm glad she can talk. I'm sure everything will return in time." Jo sighed. "Progress is a good thing. I wish JJ would wake up."

Brandon asked, "How was the hospital visit?"

"I saw the doctor yesterday. JJ's condition hasn't changed." She shrugged. "I have to believe they know what they are doing." She buckled her seatbelt, and he put the car into gear.

"Let's talk about what we will say to Tommy," she said as he pulled out of her driveway onto the road. "My sources researched the senator. He likes to take advantage of his position to make extra money and play with women behind the back of his wife. Anyone with extra time to Google could find something to blackmail the guy for. The other two appeared to be practice targets before our perp fixated on the top three names demanding huge payments."

Brandon stopped at a stop sign and faced Jo. "Tommy has three viable suspects who have been in and around Magnolia Bluff in recent days. Joyce, when she remembers, and JJ, when he wakes, may have critical information." He continued driving.

Jo smiled. "I'm glad you said when he wakes. Thanks." She huffed. "I wonder if I can get our rental car back yet. Remind me to ask, please."

"I have no issue shuttling you while we try to solve this mess," Brandon said. "Did your source find anything useful on JJ's computer? I'm surprised Tommy hasn't demanded the PC be brought in for evaluation."

"I'm not letting that happen," she insisted. "It's mine and in the house—not in the car or crime scene. My friend is working on accessing a new folder on my computer named Blackmailer, which has encrypted contents. If anything is uncovered, I'll copy the files for Tommy or show him on the machine at my house. No one gets to search JJ's machine."

Jo noticed Brandon's jaw clench and his brow furrow.

"Jo, a directory labeled blackmailer with stuff in it? I am only aware of two pieces of correspondence from the blackmailer: the hard copy of the letter you found while Tommy was there and delivery instructions for the payoff in an email with spam hiding the origin. What files would JJ have so distinctively labeled?"

"I don't know yet. My resource is trying to gain access so I can answer your question. Hopefully soon. Any comments are guesses until then. We need facts."

Brandon pulled into the police department parking lot and turned off the engine. Scanning the vicinity, he stated, "It seems a bit early for dignitaries with government plates to visit. Let's see who Tommy's talking with."

Jo grinned as she realized the possibilities. "Yes, let's."

CHAPTER 25

Damaged Egos

Brandon locked the truck door after Jo got out. They walked to the police department's entrance. Hesitating before entering due to the sounds coming from the cracked open door, Brandon commented, "Sounds like similar intense interrogation as we had at the NYPD. Someone's demanding answers. You get the best cooperation from scared teenagers but the worst cooperation from those who think they have power. I've got a hunch who's not answering to Tommy's satisfaction."

With a smirk, Jo sarcastically replied, "Mister limo with vanity plates?"

"I hope JJ doesn't get mad at me for the jaded detective attitude you're developing. Let's push in and see if you can learn new expletives to complement the detective noir you've adopted."

Jo chuckled, and they continued inside.

Brandon nodded, yet Tommy barely acknowledged them, focused on his guest. From the back, the heavy-set man had groomed salt and pepper hair under the black Stetson and a white shirt collar showing from the top of the suit jacket. Jo and Brandon sat in chairs outside the office as the conversation continued, with the intensity rising.

"There are unaccounted-for holes in your schedule, senator," Tommy loudly insisted, "here on Monday between ten in the morning and two. For the last time, WHERE WERE YOU!"

"I was with one of my constituents reviewing the schedule for the upcoming weekend." A loud BAM sounded from the man slamming his hand on the desk. "That letter is aimed at me and my household. I want it back so reporters don't rip open a can of worms to distract me from my election. You've no right to keep it from me. I've been hunting this lowlife blackmailer since I received my copy."

"It's evidence in a murder investigation, senator. You're not the only one he was threatening. Thank you for finally admitting that you have been hunting for him. When did you meet up with him? You're a suspect because of the letter and admit hunting the lowlife. Were you at 5678 Hickory Street on Monday morning during the time gap on your schedule?"

The portly man bellowed, "I just told you I was with a loyal voter. I drove myself so my aide could work on preparing for the afternoon meetings. That's what he'll tell you if you ask. I never discovered the address or the name of my blackmailer."

"That's what they all say," Tommy added accusingly.

The man sighed heavily, echoing to where Brandon and Jo sat.

"Tommy," the man whined. "Let's review the facts. I was never at that address. I never got my hand around the weasel's neck while beating him with a baseball bat. Your bogus designation as evidence for the blackmail letter addressed to me is not your concern."

With the silence, Brandon knew Tommy was coldly sizing up the man and leaned in to get the punch line.

"How did you know he was beaten with a baseball bat?"

The sounds of the man clearing his throat almost made them both chuckle. Jo clapped her hand over her mouth to maintain silence.

Tommy let the accusation linger for a few minutes. "HOW, David?" he demanded. "I'll need access to your vehicle. Sit tight and call your aide to stand outside with it unlocked. I have probable cause to search it."

Brandon overheard Tommy place the call and ask his deputy to search the limo. The silence over the next fifteen minutes was nearly unbearable before the desk phone rang, and Tommy answered, "Well?" Brandon heard Tommy's fingers drumming on the desk, then the phone set into the cradle. "My deputy said he found nothing outside of boxes of liquor and flyers, which was why it took so long."

"The water in some small towns is tainted," Senator David said, "so I bring my own. Now, how about my letter?"

"When I have a killer apprehended and the case closed," Tommy stated, "you'll get your letter back. Until then, no one will have access to it. How did you know the man was beaten with a bat, senator, and who told you about the letter? Those questions keep you on my suspect list, right on top. You're free to go. Don't leave Texas."

Noisily, the man stood and pushed back the chair into the half-wall. "Or what?" the man said. "You haven't any evidence to formally charge me, or you would have. You can't even give me a parking ticket, Chief Jager. I'm an elected official. I will proceed with my agenda of doing state business." He stomped from Tommy's office, spotting Brandon and Jo seated behind the windows.

Jo looked while the man swaggered from Tommy's office. She added her best modeling smile and coy look to her unspoken greeting. Pulled up short by Jo's beauty and pleasant smile, the senator wiped his mouth with his handkerchief and leered.

Jo graciously inclined her head in acknowledgment. "We're just waiting to speak to Chief Jager."

She watched the man puff up like a rooster, ready to strut his stuff. His practiced false courtesy showed when he picked up her hand. Jo's fingers motioned for Tommy and Brandon not to intercede.

Jo rose like a model, ready to face the media. "Are you Senator David, who's been canvassing Magnolia Bluff for votes? As a concerned voter, I'd like to know more about your platform."

He removed his dove grey Stetson and half-bowed. She was surprised not to see saliva drooling from his lips. "Ma'am, I'd be delighted to discuss my platform and show you how it stands for my constituents." He touched her arm and blouse sleeve.

Jo chuckled at the blatant innuendo. "Oh, my." She stood and leaned toward him a bit. "I've been around impressive people from all over the world, and you aren't one of them. With that oily charm, you never will be." She looked down at the unwanted hand and observed, "Sure hope I can get the grease stains out of this silk blouse." Then she walked into Tommy's office.

Senator David jammed his expensive hat back onto his head and grumbled, "Uh, bitch." Then he stormed from the building.

Tommy remained composed as Brandon chuckled.

Brandon followed Jo into Tommy's office and took a seat. Tommy closed the door, moved around the desk, and sank into his form-fitted chair. Brandon felt Tommy's piercing gaze.

"In case you weren't sure, he's one of the suspects in this investigation," commented Tommy.

Brandon innocently asked, "Did he say why he was being blackmailed? We saw the letter."

Tommy almost smiled. "Not really. He touted his concern for the well-being of the injured pair and the townsfolk. I think it comes down to removing any evidence that might incriminate him. But that's not why you're here. Tell me you found something useful."

Brandon gave a reassuring smile to a nervous Jo. "Go ahead."

She cleared her throat and sat up a little straighter. "We know why JJ was at the crime scene. He couldn't call you right away as he was given a scant ten minutes to respond to the demands via an email to our account. The instructions sent him to the Food Guys store as his first bounce point. We believe he saw this sign." Jo pulled up the picture on her phone, showed it to Tommy, and then forwarded it to his cell number. "We suspect he dropped an envelope containing a USB drive with the cryptocurrency demanded into the community collection box at the food store. Based on the broken back door Brandon found on the box, the blackmailer likely retrieved it."

Tommy's eyes widened. "He dropped a device with a hundred grand on it into a collection box? Wow. So, then he followed the guy? How? The blackmailer wouldn't have recovered it if JJ remained in the parking lot. That area has wide visibility, especially in the early morning."

Brandon interceded. "I think he added a tracking device of some sort."

Tommy nodded. "Okay. That allowed JJ to follow Rawley to his house. He could have called me then."

"Possibly," Jo admitted. "But he would have been focused on at least getting answers before alerting you."

Tommy tilted his head as if evaluating the information. "What happened to the envelope and the contents? We went all over that site with a fine-tooth comb. Nothing like that was discovered. We could go back and search the entire place again."

Brandon suggested, "Based on the gas leak, someone else was there around the same time, probably after JJ was busy talking to Rawley. But the timing is unknown. However, I would bet that person or persons took the envelope and Rawley's laptop."

Tommy stared at Jo and demanded, "JJ was simply going to pay the blackmailer and let it go?"

Jo wrinkled her brow. "Tommy, I told you, I don't know what he was planning. But we don't have that kind of money, especially after building the new home."

Tommy acknowledged, "True that. Building a new house is the greatest money-reducing event known to this generation."

"He could have used the USB as a convincing gesture. The blackmailer would not know until he opened the file."

CHAPTER 26

Paid in Full

Out on the Interstate at a pricey motel, smoke filled the air as a man pounded the keys on the computer while puffing on cigarettes. Another man periodically looked out the window to the parking lot. Both men were dressed in worn jeans and rumpled tee-shirts. The graying hair of one suggested he was twenty years older than the other.

"No one's outside, boss."

"Good. I'm not worried. We weren't seen." He refocused his attention on the machine. He got over his anger with the folder's contents bearing his name, knowing the man could never threaten him or anyone again. He decided the contents of the other folders could be a windfall for his bank account. He mentally mulled what he knew. *Even using the password for the machine extracted from that useless hacker, exposing the contents of these password-protected folders is tedious. I discovered the one for my folder with my program.* He took another drag. *They include a part of the file name because the jerk's files are organized, like a bookshelf. But, damn, each password consists of a quirky element of numbers, like a date.*

The David folder was the active target of his efforts. He launched his program to make it find the password, using the logic he learned from gaining access to his folder. The results would take a while for his digital brute force application to run.

Meanwhile, he turned his attention to the envelope containing the USB drive.

"The fool was careful but not perfect," groused the older man. "He had a junior hacker mentality and no backbone, whining like a baby. I'll have all his research, and his victims will become mine. We have an unexpected gold mine."

"If anyone can get the information, it's you," replied the younger man.

He studied the envelope with the USB drive and commented, "I bet someone paid the ransom demand. Rawley wouldn't have marked anything as paid or given his targets much of a break. I wonder which victim it was."

The laptop chirp interrupted his thoughts and indicated the first round of file opening was a success. "Good, I'm in. I can tweak the program and gain access to this treasure trove. We can play his game even better. But this device could have our stake in the future, based on Rawley's stupid demand of me." He turned the possible small goldmine over a few more times, his curiosity increasing to compel his actions. "I'll plug in this USB drive and look at how much. There might be clues as to which of the six files on the machine caved and paid."

He plugged the device into the PC, but nothing showed after it was connected. "Damn, no files registered on the machine, but I hear the drive spinning. There's nothing on here." He clucked his tongue and lit another smoke. "I took it from his shirt pocket when the discussion ended. It was protected with care and close to his black heart." He yanked it out, extended it to the other man, and ordered, "Put it into your machine and try reading it. Perhaps this USB port was disabled. I don't want to waste time trying to restore it."

The younger man completed the task and frowned. "Same result. Nada."

Losing his temper, the grey-haired man yanked the USB drive out of the machine. "Another damn puzzle," he groused while rebooting Rawley's laptop.

The other man's machine did an automatic restart.

"This can't be a blank USB drive. Why was he keeping it in his pocket if nothing was on it? That makes no sense."

Suddenly, both machines lit up in rapid succession and displayed the same scrolling message.

> You blackmailing bastard. Your machine is mine.
> I've encrypted your files.
> Your user ID is gone. You belong to me.

The older man roared, "The device contained a virus. Damn. I'm glad I didn't put it in my machine."

Trying to remain calm, the young man suggested, "I bet it's like the ransomware viruses I've built to extort funds when people foolishly click on the buttons they get offered in emails. Give me a few minutes to try some things."

The minutes dragged on until he pushed back from his machine and stood looking at his mentor. "Wow, whoever wrote this virus is good. All the normal trap doors are sealed. Every trick I know fails. I cannot access anything or think of a way around the problem. The virus taunts me back with *HET*. Was your idiot trying to blackmail an NSA virus engineer or something? He was dumb enough to try it on us, but whoever built this virus probably teaches hacking."

The older man slammed his fist on the desktop and caught the edge of the overflowing ashtray, sending the contents around the area, and bellowed, "Are you telling me, after all the viruses you've built that helped bring us millions, you can't fix it?"

He nodded. "The USB defeated the virus scanning software and installed an excellent ransomware program. But that wasn't the end game. One of Rawley's victims was good enough to anticipate and beat all the standard processes. He wanted to negotiate with the blackmailer up close and personal like you did."

"I'm suddenly famished. I'm going to clean up, then find something to eat. Maybe I'll learn something. You stay here." He rose and went toward the bathroom, then paused. "After you clean up, check out of this place and find another hotel closer to Fredericksburg. Pindrop the location to my phone. Don't use that USB drive on my laptop. Secure it while I determine how to learn the program's author."

Brayson had been working for hours remotely on JJ's computer, looking for clues from his work terminal in Luxembourg. The unexpected incoming message to JJ's machine caused him to double-take. With JJ in the hospital and Jo rarely on the machine, the inbound messaging was uncharacteristic. He held his breath and thought, "unless…" Then, second and third messages appeared.

Brayson grinned and commented, "Buddy, it looks like a beaconing signal you created to call back to your machine. This isn't one of our customers, or you would have echoed the signal on my machine. This must be something personal." He laughed. "But I don't think it is a timer alert for using a coupon at a thrift store. Let's look at the contents. Hmm, I see IP addresses and GPS locational tracking. Interesting." He rubbed his hands together like a man sitting at a Sunday feast. "If I double check the file program in the blackmail directory…yep, it's a homing program designed to send specific data to your machine. Good one, JJ."

The messaging stopped, meaning the sender's machine was shut down. Brayson hunted on JJ's machine and opened the small text file in the blackmail sub-directory. The contents read–

> The cloaking program will lock up the host machine, so nothing
> will operate except my beaconing program. Expect to get a
> few beaconing signals before the blackmailer realizes the USB
> drive is poisoned. Either the blackmailer machine alerts me to
> its location, or they seek me out for an antidote. As soon as
> the beaconing begins, I own the machine, and they are out of
> business until they agree to my demands.

Brayson felt sad and lamented, "JJ, it was a great plan until it wasn't. The blackmailer is dead, and you're in a coma." He shook off his sadness. "If the blackmailer's dead, where's the signal coming from?"

CHAPTER 27

Not to Worry, I'll Handle It

Frowning at the incoming face of his talented but needy musical client. Her pretty face was framed with dark curls and piercing green eyes. Johnnie resignedly sighed. "Hey, Abby, what's up?"

"Did you clean up the mess? Is the ransom demand paid? And when will I get the photos back?"

Though her singing voice was like an angel's and her stage presence dynamic, Abby was the most demanding of his clients. He would have cut her loose if she didn't earn over fifty percent of his annual income. He rolled his eyes and forced a smile into his voice as he replied, "Nothing's been confirmed yet on the meeting place, so I haven't sent anything. The blackmailer hasn't replied. I'm taking a wait-and-see attitude."

Abby shrieked, "That's just great. As my agent, you're supposed to take care of this."

He heard her pacing and slamming doors to vent frustration. "Abby, relax; it'll be fine."

"What are you, nuts? They're not pictures of a politician handling your boobs that someone's threatening to post on social media. My mama would die if those came out. You told me to pose for some publicity shots with him." She inhaled loudly and sipped on something. "I did what you asked; then he insisted we go for a drink after the show to *thank me!*"

It was impossible not to miss the scorn in her voice, and he felt partly responsible.

"No one was around when he ripped my new custom-designed, purple sequined bodice with one of his roving hands. Thank goodness he didn't do worse before I used the moves my brothers taught me and screamed at him to leave. Don't ever book a show for me in Texas again, Johnnie."

"Abby, you're sold out for two nights. The fans loved you; the press couldn't rave enough about your songs. You're getting the career traction you wanted. The senator endorsed you, sent an apology note to you, and reimbursed you for the clothing he inadvertently ruined. We can't fret about a blackmail threat unless they make contact. Focus on the next show. Let me deal with this."

"The blackmailer is probably betting I'll hit the big time and demand more. You got me into it, Johnnie. I want those photos," Abby cried.

Growing weary, he soothed, "We'll cross that bridge when we come to it. Toss this one off as a wardrobe malfunction. Focus on the next concert. The traction in Texas is helping with your show in Phoenix. They asked me if you could add another night because the stadium was sold out in an hour."

"Really? I can do another night or maybe a matinee for the younger crowd on Sunday."

Johnnie nodded. "That's my star. I like the idea, Abby, of a Sunday afternoon. Do you want me to book it if they agree?"

"Yes. Thanks. I guess that's why you're the booking agent. I'll stop whining and go back to work."

Johnnie disconnected and muttered, "Note to self: stay away from politicians."

Senator David rolled the USB drive between his thumb and index finger, almost like playing with a fidget spinner. This little device held his future.

"Senator," his aide asked, "do you need anything else this afternoon?"

Glancing toward his newest intern, he grinned. "No, you can take a break. I want to review a list of my new campaign donors who can't wait to contribute. I need to figure out the best way to approach them. Pick me up at five thirty so we can be on time at the Lakeway Women's League dinner."

The aide appeared confused. "Okay. I can help you with it. I had no idea you had a new list."

He waved his hand in dismissal. "I got this. You go on."

After hearing the outer door close, he powered up his laptop. While waiting, he thought, *reading through a list of people who, until I call with my pitch, have no idea they want to contribute is almost magical.*

He struggled to slide the device into the side slot with his beefy digits. The information window showed the contents. He clicked on one of the files and grinned as it opened, revealing the prized results. "I'm glad I retrieved this drive from Rawley before he died," muttered David. "With these names and a little prodding, I'll get in the race for the U.S. Senate next year." Pausing momentarily and holding up a tumbler of water like a microphone, he announced, "Introducing U.S. Senator David from Texas. I like the sound of that."

He scrolled through the list of names and addresses. He read the notes on why they would contribute and licked his lips, trying to taste victory. Then he sorted the list by zip code, recognizing a few names in and around Magnolia Bluff. "As long as I need to stay close to the area to appease Chief Jager, I might as well work on my new sponsors. I'll start tonight." He smirked. "It won't be the first time I've received votes and donations from people I've insulted. That part of campaigning has always come easy to me."

CHAPTER 28

When was the Last Time?

Lily saw him from the edge of the dining room as he confidently strode through the front door in pressed jeans, a tailored cowboy shirt with pearl buttons, and alligator boots. When their eyes met, he gave her a subtle grin and held up a package. Intrigued by the handsome man with longish black sprinkled-with-grey hair, she wondered if she would be hustled for something since it was past her breakfast service. His chiseled face and dark eyes seemed familiar. She closed the distance between them, ready to tell him the kitchen was closed when she recognized him.

"I remember, you're the Russian feller from last week. I'm sorry I don't recall your name, but I never forget a face."

Raising his hand, he proclaimed, "Dostoevsky, madam innkeeper. I remember your charming conversation from last time. Please call me Boris."

Lily chuckled and picked up the side of her apron in a half-curtsy. "Nice to get your name, Boris. You can call me Lily. My helper is at school, and my breakfast rush ended a while ago. I was finishing the setup for later. Harry's Really Good café should open for lunch at eleven if you're hungry."

Boris waved off the suggestion, settled into a chair at an empty table, and, in his deep baritone voice, announced, "Ms. Lily, food is not important at the moment. You entertained me with lively conversation while I enjoyed a delicious meal. You made me laugh like a friend. In true Russian tradition, I'm compelled to return the gesture." He grinned and waggled his eyebrows. "Do you still have some of that marvelous orange juice?" He pulled a bottle of vodka from the paper bag and placed it on the table. "Perhaps you might spare some time to practice your Russian and share my contribution to mix with the tangy liquid?"

Chortling, Lily took two glass tumblers, napkins, and spoons from the sideboard and set them on the table. "Let me get a cold pitcher of orange juice from the refrigerator. I'll be right back." At the swinging door, she turned her head and said over her shoulder, "No getting me crocked on vodka before noon. I've too many things to do today."

Boris laughed and raised a hand. "My intentions are mostly honorable. I'm a stranger to this country but have found Texas more interesting since I met you."

Lily returned, set the metal container on the table, and sat. "I must admit, Boris, this is odd for me. It's been long since anyone's showed up here to visit." She tapped the side of the bottle with her index finger. "Especially with a Russian beverage."

She watched his powerful hands ease out the cork as he dismissed her comment.

"I have few people with whom I enjoy sharing a conversation or confidence. I must reach out when I see one who should be a treasured friend."

He carefully combined the two components, and she noted equal amounts of vodka in each glass. Taking a spoon, he mixed them and gestured for her to take one.

He raised his glass. "To a fine lady born in Texas with the heart of a Russian. *Nah zda-ROVH-yeh!*"

Lily clicked his glass and took a sip. "Boris, teach me to say that."

After half a dozen attempts, she could not wrap her tongue around the letters to correct the sound. "I can't do it. I'll teach you a Texas toast." Lily raised her glass. "*Come and take it!*"

She chuckled at the blank look on his face. "It was the Texans' challenge to the Mexican soldiers at the Battle of Gonzales during the Texas Revolution in 1835." Realizing the excellent vodka could go to her head if she weren't mindful, she said, "Let me get us some cookies to go with your delightful concoction."

Placing a plate of cookies between them, they laughed, talked about history, and discussed several other topics over two drinks for nearly an hour. Lily experienced lightheadedness and tingling in her fingers as he prepared their third.

"I've had enough for today. Now that we are friends…" she hiccupped and felt the flush rise on her cheeks. "What else do you want to talk about while you're being so honorable?"

Boris's eyes twinkled, feigning innocence. "Does that mean a romantic interlude is a possibility? Ms. Lily, I only ask since you fill out a dress in a way that sparks a man's imagination."

Lily didn't know what to say for the first time in forever. She studied his expression, looking for answers. Then he surprised her.

"When did a gentleman caller last take you out to dinner? I envision lively company with spirited banter between us. You are saucy, petite, funny, and…pretty. Allow me the privilege of escorting you for a night out."

Lily was stunned and immediately sober. In all her years of running Flower and the many guests who had passed through the doors, no man had asked her out since her husband died. She swallowed hard. "I…don't know what to say. Isn't that hilarious? I've not been out since my husband…" She suddenly felt pretty. The musky scent of his cologne was enticing. Her pulse unexpectedly quickened.

Boris's eyes met hers. He gently took her hand and leaned forward to brush it with a kiss, his old-world charm irresistible enough to make her tremble.

He broke the silence, then confidently stated, "I'll come for you at six this evening. Wear something special I won't ever forget." He stood. "Until then, adieu."

She watched him and sat motionless, her inebriated mind swirling with possibilities.

CHAPTER 29

Date Night

Brandon parked the truck in Joyce's driveway and pocketed the keys. He sat motionless in the seat and blew out a long breath. "Whew. I thought I retired, but now I'm back at it and chauffeuring damsels in distress." He chuckled, knowing he wouldn't change a thing.

He entered via the front door with the key Joyce provided. "Hey, Max. Do you remember me, old buddy?"

Max came boiling from the kitchen with Joyce not far behind. Moving like a runaway freight train, the excited pup rushed over the wooden floor, picked up a small throw rug with his paws, and skidded into Brandon, nearly knocking him to the floor. They greeted one another for a minute like they'd been separated for weeks rather than a few hours.

Joyce laughed at the scene. "Max is my best buddy until you arrive. Then it's Joyce, who?"

Brandon smiled at her. "You've still got your voice. That's great." He ran a hand over Max's head. "He does the same thing when I bring him here and runs to find you or Jason." He gave her a quick hug. "It's been a day. How about we escape for the evening? I'll take you to dinner and celebrate your recovery. We'll have Jason puppy-sit, and he can order in his favorite."

"That's a great idea. When Jason came home about a half hour ago, he indicated that he had homework." She looped her arm around his, and they started for the kitchen, a favorite place to sit and talk. "I believe you've been ordering in since the incident occurred," she said with a slight rasp. "But I love the idea. I wouldn't mind getting dressed up and enjoying a night out. Maybe some tongue-waggers will see me and stop speculating. I called my boss and said I would be at work on Saturday." Joyce poured them each a glass of tea. "What restaurant did you have in mind? Something upscale like the Silver Spoon, or a little more downhome cooking like Lily's Flower B&B?"

He considered the options and mentally reviewed the menus. "How about the Silver Spoon? The setting is nice, with music in the background, and the service is always good. Lily makes great food, but she recently did the barbecue. I want something different."

"Your decision process for dining cracks me up. Let me go change." She eyed him head to toe and grinned. "You look ready to go."

"Yep, I needed to shower and change. Long day."

Joyce chuckled. "I'll be back."

While she scampered off to get ready, Brandon sipped his tea, imagining what she would wear, and wrote a note for Jason. He added some money on top. Several minutes later, Joyce glided into the kitchen wearing a pretty blue dress that complemented her light hair and highlighted her slim waist. He was glad they had found each other. "I am…uh…happy to go wherever you want, sweetie."

"The Silver Spoon is perfect," she said, then turned. "Can you please finish zipping me? My arms aren't long enough."

"Any time. Did you want that zipped up or down?"

"Up," she giggled.

"How's your memory? Any new sketches or images you were able to name?"

Not getting an answer right away, Brandon added water to the bowl on the floor and let Max outside to inspect the yard.

"Nothing new, just the same jumbled images with lights and reflections."

Brandon beamed. "They'll likely show up when you least expect them. Come on. You look lovely. I can't wait to show you off. I left Jason a message about his dinner."

"Perfect. I mentioned it to him when I went to my room. He has two projects to complete but agreed to watch Max."

Joyce smiled as she tucked some unruly hair behind his ear and offered, "Let's go check out the cloth napkins."

Laughing, they headed out.

CHAPTER 30

Have a Crayon Handy?

Jo slipped through the pergola side door into the kitchen, almost on autopilot. JJ's condition had not changed after her recent conversation with his physician. Brandon was great at taking her around, but she felt trapped. She placed her purse, keys, and phone on the counter and decided to get a new rental car if Tommy didn't release their vehicle by tomorrow afternoon. It was time she had a way to go to the hospital on demand or when she needed to see him.

The quiet was unnerving; the whiskey bottle Hank had left caught her eye. Jo shook her head. "Thank goodness I'm not prone to drink, especially alone." She rose and went to the stove to heat water for a cup of tea. Her phone rang, and Brayson's image appeared. She reached over and pressed answer. "Hi. I'm feeling down, so let's start with good news," Jo sighed.

"Ah, Jo, I'm sorry. I can't imagine how you feel, but I can still catch the next flight if you want," he offered.

"No. My friends here are keeping close and helping. I want JJ to make some improvements. The doctor said the lack of deterioration is positive. He will even let me have additional time for up to an hour in the morning and evening. At least I can hold his hand and talk to him, which might help, too." Tears blurred her vision, and she reached for a tissue. Jo began sobbing. "You're right. I'm a mess."

Brayson soothed, "How about some good news you can share with Tommy?"

Jo choked back her next sob and breathed. "I like it."

"Make your tea, I'll wait."

She laughed. "You know me too well." She poured the steaming water over the fragrant tea bag. "Thanks."

"Jo, I know what JJ had in mind. I studied the rest of the files and ran a program he left. In layman's terms, he built a core zero application that intercepts any program instructions but his. The program allowed JJ to use an elliptical encryption program to lock the files on the target machine. My best estimate is that the program can only be broken using a quantum computer to decrypt. Even then, it could take years."

"Wow. I think that's good, Brayson, but it's a bit over my head," Jo chuckled.

He sighed. "Sorry, I do get into it. It's good because nothing will recover the machine it's installed on."

Jo deadpanned, "Oh, it's a computer virus."

Brayson howled with laughter. "Whatever made you think you weren't smart enough to be in tech?" He laughed uproariously. After a breath, he added, "I've removed computer viruses for city governments, hospitals, banks, utility companies, and even dry cleaners, but JJ's virus is pure genius."

"Dry cleaners?"

"Yes. The cleaners had a huge clientele," he said.

"I feel better. Thanks. JJ built a computer virus with a beaconing element so Tommy could get directed to its location. I knew he was awesome."

"Grab your pencil, Jo. I got some coordinates you can share with Brandon and Tommy."

CHAPTER 31

Defining Moments

Brandon found the ideal parking spot at the Silver Spoon as they pulled in at six. He turned off the motor and smiled at Joyce. He placed his hand on her arm. "Keep seated, honey, while I come around for you."

"Thank you."

He hustled out of the car and rushed around to open the door. She smiled as he extended his hand to help her out. Joyce stepped down, adding a bit of soft-shoe footwork on the pavement.

Brandon whistled. "I like the dance steps and how your skirt rides up your shapely thigh. We may have to dance to a few songs later."

Joyce smoothed her dress and smiled at him. "Sounds fun."

Brandon guided her through the entrance of the Silver Spoon. They waited as the hostess seated another couple ahead of them. There were scattered diners immersed in their private conversations, but Brandon only had eyes for Joyce.

The waitress approached their table. Brandon said, "We'd like a bottle of champagne, please. We're celebrating."

The waitress smiled and turned to comply with the request.

Brandon reached over and rubbed a finger gently over Joyce's hand while they reviewed the menu. Flirtatious comments were exchanged, punctuated with bursts of laughter. Based on her eye contact, the magic of the night was intoxicating Joyce.

The waitress placed a bucket of ice surrounding the champagne and took their order. Brandon poured the glasses after she left and raised his for a toast. "Here's to your continued health and recovery, sweetie."

"Thank you for all your support."

A noisy couple entered the dining area and were seated to the side. Brandon suspected they were celebrating something as well. He heard the man's accent, thinking it was perhaps Russian. The woman seated next to him looked familiar. He did a double-take, realizing it was Lily. "Joyce, did you know Lily was dating someone?"

Joyce turned slightly to check out the couple. She shook her head. Her eyes widened. "No one's mentioned it to me. I've never seen her so dolled up, so it must be a date. Good for—" She stopped speaking and faced Brandon.

He realized something was wrong. Joyce's skin rippled with goosebumps, and her coloring paled. She turned her head to take another look and closed her eyes. He placed his hand on hers when he noticed her trembling.

"Honey, are you cold? Do you want my jacket?"

Joyce mumbled, "That man, he looks familiar." She closed her eyes again.

Brandon grew concerned when he saw her clench her fists. Her lips were taut.

Her eyes opened, and she said, "Flashes. I think it's his face. Not certain."

Worried that something about the man triggered her memory, he said, "Wait here, I'll be right back."

She nodded. "I don't want to leave."

He patted her hand. "That's good."

Unable to resist the opportunity, he stood, grabbed his phone with one hand, and approached the table. "Lily, what a surprise. It's nice to see you enjoying an evening out. Please introduce me."

Lily appeared thrilled, though her date narrowed his eyes.

"Brandon, meet Boris, my new friend from Russia. He asked me out tonight and chose here. He's ensuring I don't have another orange juice and vodka until I've eaten.

Confused, Brandon looked at the man. "Hello, Boris, good to meet you."

Lily slurred, "Are you here with Joyce? How is she?" She leaned to look around him but didn't get the direction right.

Brandon smirked at her speech and exaggerated movements, realizing she was borderline wasted but happy. "Yes, but we're leaving soon. I must take a photo. You two make a charming couple."

Lily laughed and leaned into Boris. "Only if you send it to me."

Boris held up his hand and stated, "HET."

It was too late, so Brandon shrugged. "Sorry. Lily, thanks for all the support you've given this town. I'll send you a copy. Boris, it's so nice to meet you. Do you have a phone? I can push the photo to it."

Brandon saw the man glare but ignored the hostility. "I'm sorry to have intruded. Please stay and enjoy your meal." He headed to his table, but Joyce was gone. He scanned the area. When he couldn't spot her, he stopped the waitress.

"Did you see which way my date went?"

"Sir, she said she had to leave and would speak to you later. The manager put her in a ride-share. I hope you don't mind; we added it to your bill."

He shook his head, frowning, and handed her his credit card. "No problem."

CHAPTER 32

More or Less

Lily lost her buzz when she watched Boris's eyes follow Brandon's departure. She tried to re-energize their mood before the interruption. "I am ready to order. How about you?"

Boris swallowed half his drink in one gulp. His expression was serious when he nodded to get the waitress's attention. "Of course. What are you having?"

"I'd like to have the pork chop and scalloped potatoes. I rarely serve it, so it'll be a treat," she grinned.

He didn't make eye contact and tapped his fingers against his drink, almost brooding. She wondered how to recapture the fun when he agreed, "Sounds like I should try it too. Your friend Brandon seemed too interested in your business to me."

Lily laughed and reached across to touch his arm. "Oh, Boris, this small town is filled with people who know everyone's business. He retired here and is dating a lovely friend of mine. Joyce has been feeling poorly this week, and I suspect they wanted a night out to forget her short stint in the hospital."

She noticed his interest pique when he raised an eyebrow. She added, "I need to call her tomorrow and check how she's doing."

"I hope she is well. Perhaps we should send a drink to their table," he suggested.

"No, I don't want to share our time with them. Tell me about you."

Boris steepled his hands. "I had a small issue with my computer earlier today. I think it received a virus, but I don't know how it happened. I looked for a local repair shop but found nothing nearby."

Frowning, she commented, "I had no idea you were a computer expert. Is it part of your livelihood?"

The waitress interrupted their discussion and took their order.

He recited meal choices and added another drink. When she left, he waved off Lily's last comment with a flick of his fingers. "I do research using the internet. My computer is important to my work."

"We have a terrific library in town, and they have walk-up computers for that use. Caroline, my friend, works there." Lily nudged him with her elbow. "Tell her I sent you, and she'll waive the fee."

"You have many friends, it would seem. People tell you things and share stories. What will Brandon do with the picture?"

Lily cocked her head, wondering about the question. "Nothing outside of sharing with Joyce and perhaps a few friends who won't believe I was out with someone as handsome as you." She looked around at the pretty pictures on the walls, white tablecloths, uniformed waitstaff, and animated couples deep in conversation over delicious plates of food. "I haven't had dinner here in years. Thank you for choosing such a lovely venue."

He smiled at her, and she noticed it didn't reach his eyes. Dinner was served, shifting the conversation to silence. Her concern grew because his cheerful, intimate attitude was missing. When he looked toward her, his dark eyes appeared troubled, deep in thought.

"Tell me about your friends, pretty lady," he said with renewed interest. "I saw a newspaper article that someone had died recently. I hope that was not one of your friends."

Hoping the awkwardness was behind them, she replied, "Oh, mercy, no. Thankfully. However, several of my friends were impacted. For instance, Joyce and Jo are dealing with some serious things." She leaned, bumped his shoulder, and added, in a conspiratorial tone, "Joyce rented the property to the victim."

"Joe, who's he?" he demanded. "Should I be jealous of your affection for another?"

She chuckled. "Jo is a dear girl I love like a daughter. Her husband suffered an accident of sorts and lies in a coma." Growing melancholy, she added, "Can we talk about something else? I want to learn more Russian."

"And I want to hear more about your friends and how the killing affected them."

Lily felt his eyes boring into her. The food she'd just eaten soured in her belly, and the vodka finally gave her a headache. Something about his directness and insistence made her jittery. "Boris, I'm sorry, I'm feeling ill. Can you please take me home?"

His frustration showed as he slammed his napkin onto the table and raised his hand to get the waitress's attention. "Let me pay the bill. I'll drop you at your house, but we'll talk tomorrow." He squeezed her hand a bit too tightly. "Now that I am your friend, I want to learn more about your friends."

He dropped her at Flower's front door and dismissively said, "I will see you tomorrow."

Lily rushed inside, disappointed at no goodnight kiss. Walking like her feet had lead weights, she locked the doors, glad she had no overnight guests. Confused, she plopped down in an overstuffed flowered print chair, trying to recall everything she'd told Boris. "Sometimes you can't stop your mouth from running, can you, Lily," she muttered. Something felt off. The unexpected knock on the door had her sharply inhale and freeze. Concerned it might be Boris, she remained quiet, knowing she was hidden in the shadows of the front room.

A more insistent knock sounded, then a familiar voice.

Boris watched Lily let herself into Flower and slammed his hands on the steering wheel, angry that he was not getting all the information he wanted. He drove to the center of Magnolia Bluff and texted Mikhail.

> Where are we sleeping tonight?

The response took an annoying minute.

> I found two adjoining rooms at the Wyndham Inn near Fredericksburg, about half an hour from you.

Boris entered the coordinates into his map, hit start for the directions to appear, and snarled, "Forty-two minutes!"

> Why two rooms? Did you get rich?

He noticed an indication that Mikhail was typing.

> They only had one bed, but they are full-size.

When he arrived at the hotel, his anger had cooled. He knocked on the door to the appropriate room, and Mikhail let him in.

"Where's my laptop?"

"In your room, Boss." He pointed to the adjoining doorway, which stood open.

Boris ambled in, glad that his clothes were hung in the closet. He spotted the no-smoking sign and frowned. "You couldn't find a room that allowed smoking?"

Mikhail leaned against the doorway. "Not for miles. I tried. There is one on the interstate about a hundred miles away, but you indicated we needed to remain nearby. I took a ride-share here rather than borrowing another car."

"Any luck in getting your project completed?"

"I haven't tried since I arrived here. They have a business area in the lobby. I researched the free computers and downloaded a possible solution."

"Then get to it. I need to access the internet myself. Did you order dinner?"

"Yes, sir. I ate."

"Goodnight then."

Boris heard Mikhail close the door as he entered the bathroom to shower before starting work.

CHAPTER 33

Can We Talk?

Jo phoned Brandon after getting all the information from Brayson. He answered immediately but breathlessly asked, "Are you all right?"

"I'm good. I have some information we might want to share with Tommy. Where are you? Is Joyce all right? I thought I heard sobbing when you answered."

Brandon sighed. "I'm at Joyce's. We went to dinner at the Silver Spoon. She saw something that upset her. I think it is triggering her memories. She went to lie down after I said you were calling."

"I hate to take you away from her," said Jo, biting her lip and weighing her options.

"It's okay. We've been going through it for half an hour. She's exhausted. I'll stick around here on the couch tonight. I want to be close if she wakes up. Tell me what you have. My ears are working."

She smiled. "My source spotted a beaconing signal traced to a program JJ wrote to attack a machine like a virus. It calls home, like a lost, chipped puppy, as long as it's powered on. I have the geocoordinates from that signal earlier today."

"That's cool. Wow, a signpost to show the way. Can you text them to me? I'll share them with Tommy as a possible lead that I'll explain later."

Jo grinned, sensing positive action toward taking JJ off the suspect list. "I'll text them now. Let me know when they arrive."

Jo sighed through the silence.

"Okay, Jo. I have them. I'll take care…"

Jo heard Joyce call out. "Brandon, I think I need your help to…"

"Jo, I gotta go. Call you after I reach Tommy."

Tommy heard footsteps before the entrance to Flower burst open. Lily slammed into him, knocking him breathless. "Oof."

He moved her inside, closed the door, and eyed her head to toe. "I don't know what's more unsettling: you crashing into me or seeing you dressed like Cinderella. You're home before midnight, so the tears mean we must find your glass slipper? Am I close?"

Lily stepped back into the entry space, where the outdoor light illuminated the area by the check-in desk. Her tear-streaked face had him stroking her arm, unexpectedly concerned. "Lily, I didn't expect to interrupt your drama. I came over to talk about my issues. I've never seen you like this. What happened?"

Wiping her tears with a soggy tissue, she could hardly speak without blubbering. "Tommy, it was a perfect day. He came courting. We flirted most of the morning. He insisted we go to dinner and celebrate our new friendship. I haven't spent that much time putting on makeup and doing wardrobe changes to impress a man in years."

Tommy reached the check-in desk counter, snagged a couple of fresh tissues, and handed them over.

She nodded, dried her eyes, and hiccupped. "Thanks. I was in hog heaven with the lavish attention when he picked me up.

At one point, I was certain we'd be in his back seat at the reservoir like a couple of teenagers."

Tommy tilted his head, confused. "Who's your new flame? I've heard nothing in the grapevine about you dating."

Lily inhaled, appearing to gain control. "Everything was fine until Brandon showed up at our table and took a photo before we could object. He said I looked pretty, then promised to text us the picture. Boris lost his temper when I tried to discuss us. He wanted to talk about this guy—" she did an air quote with her fingers— "Brandon, who took pictures of us, then Boris asked questions about everyone I knew. When he mentioned the newspaper story, suddenly it all felt wrong."

Tommy watched as the emotion swelled across her features again.

She sniffled. "The next thing I knew, he was on the passenger side and walked me to the door. He said he'd return tomorrow to talk about my friends. Then he drove off."

Tommy pulled Lily into his arms as she sobbed. Suddenly, she pushed him off and bolted toward the restroom. Concerned, he followed her as she leaned over the commode. A few minutes later, he handed her a cool washcloth for her face.

"We can sit and talk if you want."

Lily nodded and leaned against Tommy as they approached the dining room. He guided her to the first table and pulled out her chair.

"Sorry for the remark about losing your glass slipper. Let's turn on the lights. I'll grab things from the kitchen and be right back."

Concerned and confused by this side of Lily, he picked out club soda, reheated a cup of coffee, and grabbed a plate of cookies. Out of his comfort zone, he wondered where this discussion would head.

They sat in silence for several minutes. Lily stared at the table, nursing her sparkling water. He presumed she was looking for answers.

She blurted, "Thanks for being the one at my door." She raised her eyes to his and added, "I appreciate your holding my hair back while I threw up. I feel better now."

Tommy shrugged. "That's what friends are for."

Lily's bottom lip protruded, looking like a child sent home from school. "You know how my day went. Why are you here? You mentioned we needed to talk."

"I've been trying to keep a lid on some of the crime details. Things I thought weren't public keep surfacing. The underlying rumors and gossip are remarkably accurate. I revealed some information to you with a request to keep it to yourself. Have you provided any details to the gossip tree?"

Lily jerked her head, facing him with eyes blazing. "Tommy, you told me to put a sock in it until you solved the crime. I told you I would. I'm a talker, but I don't go back on my word. I've heard a few things I was going to mention, though." She straightened her shoulders and glared. "You know what I tell them? *You don't say.* That's it."

His phone vibrated in his pocket. He held up a finger and grabbed it to check, finding a text from Brandon: "Just a second, Lily, I need to do something with this message. Do you have any sandwich-making ingredients in the back? I'm hungry."

Lily walked toward the kitchen with grace and a slow glide.

He grinned as he called Brandon. "Hey, man. I just read your text. Thanks for the info. Where did it come from?"

"I'll tell ya later. Joyce is having issues. I think maybe she's recalling some events. Check out the beacon, and if there is a laptop, it's likely Rawley's."

"I'll put Reece on it."

"Dang, wait a second. I have some different coordinates than before. Use these, Tommy. I'll call you if I get anything more."

"Thanks, Brandon." Tommy disconnected. He sent a text and then phoned Reece.

Tommy curtly said, "I received a lead on the laptop at the location I just texted you. Go check it out."

"Tonight? It's late."

"Yes. It may break open our case. You can get credit," insisted Tommy.

"Okay. I'll go."

"Call me when you get something."

"Yes, sir."

Lily returned with a roast beef sandwich and some chips. "Here you go, Tommy. With mayonnaise and lettuce, no tomato." She sat.

"Yummy," Tommy indicated after the first bite. "Sorry about asking you, but I had to check. I'm trying to solve a murder, and to make matters worse…well, never mind. The list of suspects is shortening at least." He patted her hand. "Let's change the subject. Do I need to do anything about Boris? Your instincts are usually spot-on. If you're frightened by him…"

A little indignant, Lily protested, "I'm armed since you made me take handgun training. If he returns, I'll deal with it and call you."

Tommy furrowed his brow. "Oh great, another pending homicide. I'll probably swing by here often for coffee roadies so I can be here if he shows up to badger you."

Lily smiled and leaned over to kiss his cheek. "You aren't fooling anyone, my friend. You like my coffee and breakfast tacos."

CHAPTER 34

Play Ball or Lose

Reece grumbled about Tommy as he hit the two-lane highway. "Nine o'clock at night, trying to find something beaconing from Fredericksburg. Geesh! I swear he does this to get me out of the way." He turned into a fast-food restaurant's drive-through and ordered a large coffee. "Humph," he complained as he followed the GPS route, finally pulling into the hotel parking lot in a space close to the entrance.

Frowning, Reece got out of the car and locked it, then stood there studying the two-story structure. "How the heck will I determine the exact location of the stupid signal? I bet this place has a hundred rooms." Reece's brainstorms were like drizzle, messy but not overflowing. He muttered, "The signal is new in this location, according to Tommy, so they must be recent guests. A flash of my badge will get the new check-ins."

Reece approached the counter. "I need to know the names and room numbers of guests who checked in today."

The receptionist spoke broken English. "I can't give private information."

Reece flashed his badge. "It's police business, ma'am."

The receptionist shook her head. After several back-and-forth comments, Reece insisted he speak to the duty manager. She dialed the requested person and handed the phone to Reece.

A man answered, "I'm the manager. How can I help you?"

"I have a person of interest connected to a crime in Magnolia Bluff somewhere in your hotel. I must speak to them. I asked for the people who checked in today, but your staff is unwilling to give me that information."

"Rightly so. We don't give out that guest information without a warrant. I don't know about these geolocators, but the data at the end of the string is used to identify the user and their room number while in our hotel. We had folks pirating our guest Wi-Fi access. To stop it, we added check-in and -out dates with room numbers to the data string to verify they're paying guests. Hand the phone back to my clerk, please."

The receptionist listened to her boss and typed into her terminal. She wrote information onto a notepad and handed it to Reece.

He grinned at the results. "Thank you, ma'am."

Reece grabbed the open elevator and went to the second floor. He approached the first of the two rooms on the paper. "They assign rooms in numerical order; how funny," he murmured. He selected a fresh cigar from his pocket, unwrapped it, and stuck it into the usual jaw side of his face. Then, he placed the wrapper into his pocket to dispose of later.

He assumed his macho-detective character and pounded on door number two-twenty-five thrice. A man in his late thirties cracked open the door and, in a thick accent, asked, "Problem?"

"I must come in and speak with you," Reece demanded.

The young man shook his head and stuttered, "No Englisia."

Knowing he had a fifty-pound advantage and training, Reece shoved on the door, forcing the small, wiry man back, and entered the room.

Scanning the room, Reece asked, "Do you have any computer equipment?"

The man raised his hands, palms up, shook his head, and rolled his shoulders. He pointed to his chest with his thumb and said one word. "Lithuanian."

Frustrated, Reece was considering his options when his cell phone rang. He looked at the screen and spotted Tommy's picture. He answered, "Yeah, Chief, this guy says he doesn't speak English. He looks harmless."

"Nice work, Reece," the chief said. "You've located the beaconing signal. It went off again, and you appeared right on top of it. Who is it?"

Reece grinned and eyed the man suspiciously. He placed the phone on a low table and activated speaker mode. "Give me that again. This guy says he's Lithuanian and doesn't speak English."

Reece looked around the room, spotting a laptop on a table near the window. He looked at the man and demanded, "Do you have a computer in this room?"

The man shook his head, shrugged, raised his hands, then realized his error. He tried to push past Reece to escape.

Reece slammed his stocky body into the man, knocking him to the floor beside the bed. In seconds, the handcuffs connected. He yanked the man into a sitting position on the bed.

Reece pulled his weapon and aimed it at the man's heart. "International language at work," laughed the detective.

"I found the PC, chief. There are two, but only one is turned on. Despite his claims, Mr. Lithuanian seems to understand English. I'll meet you at the station." Reece disconnected the call and smirked. "Chalk up another win for the Sovern."

Reece tucked the laptop under his arm, grasped the handcuff chain, and escorted the man toward the elevator. Hearing the door to the next room close and the lock set, Reece figured this hotel's walls were too thin but didn't apologize for disturbing the guests.

Boris took care as he double-locked his room. He waited an eternity for the sounds of the people to vanish. He peeked through the crack and saw no one. He heaved the pillow, towel, and every item not nailed down, then stomped the floor. "Unbelievable," he growled. Mikhail won't say a word, I know. Still, this whole thing is a mess."

He sat at his laptop and researched Magnolia Bluff for Joyce and realtors. "Finally, a break," he said. The local newspaper article commended their new top salesperson at the area's biggest little real estate office. "She's a superstar with a memorable face. Damnit. Perhaps way too conscientious in checking on her buyers," he announced. "I hate loose ends."

Vladimir assembled his clothes and laptop bags, setting them by the door. Then he went through the adjoining door, packed Mikhail's stuff, and carried it to his room. He locked the connecting door from his side. The auto check-out using the TV took a second; he left down the back stairs and exited to the parking lot. If anyone returned, he'd rather doze in his car than get caught in the room.

After loading the car, he drove to an all-night truck stop, parked between two eighteen-wheelers, and curled up to rest in the backseat. The drone of the idling diesel engines lulled him. His last thoughts were of visiting Lily first thing in the morning. He promised, "I will win!"

CHAPTER 35

Making Brownie Points

Reece chuckled to himself as he headed down the road toward Magnolia Bluff. Pleased with the results from a questionable assignment, he rolled the caller index to a well-used phone number. The call was immediately answered.

"I lucked out and retrieved Rawley's laptop," he said, "so you can stop fretting. I'm en route to deliver that item and the Lithuanian culprit to Tommy's jail." After a few moments of listening, he asked, "I still don't understand what this guy had on you and why you couldn't explain it to the chief…I know you're essential…I realize you're looking out for the interest of Magnolia Bluff, or you wouldn't know anything…No, you can't just show up tomorrow and demand the PC be destroyed because Tommy will ask, *'How do you know about that*?' He's obstinate, not stupid…

Reece shifted in his seat, holding in an exasperated sigh.

"I can't do that either. He knows I have the damn thing. Someone put tracking software on it so we could locate it. If I start it up, it will beacon again while in your hands, so no…Look, you asked for my help as a fellow Texan. I believed your sob story. I've helped you. Stop over-amping on accessing the machine… What do you mean, I'd better play ball? Show up, ask for a briefing, and see where that leads…I've gotten you as far as possible, so don't be so heavy-handed…Good. Much more practical. Talk later."

He disconnected, frowned, and eyed the culprit behind the plexiglass with disdain.

CHAPTER 36

Turn the Page

At dark thirty, Tommy arrived at Flower for coffee. The street out front was quiet. He saw illumination inside, so he knew Lily was up. He knocked on the door. He saw her shadow and called, "Lily, it's Tommy. Open up."

The key turned in the lock, and she swung open the door. "Coffee's on." She turned and headed for the kitchen. He locked up and followed her.

"How'd you sleep?" he asked as he entered the kitchen.

"Not so hot. I've got a sick headache and promised myself never to drink vodka again."

He laughed. "Good call. Whiskey's better."

"Are ya hungry?"

"Sure, if you have some of your fabulous sweet rolls."

Lily smiled, pulled a plate of cinnamon rolls from the oven, and added some whipped butter on the side.

"Thanks. Has Boris called or stopped by?"

"No. I have entrances locked and my gun in my pocket." She tapped her apron. "I put the safety back on when you announced yourself."

"Good girl." He took a bite. "Mmm." Chewing a moment, he added, "Best ones ever."

"You always say that." She grinned as she cracked eggs for morning breakfast.

"They get better every time. It's not my fault; it's your skill. Lily, I want you to close Flower for the day. We jailed a man last night whom I need to question. I have a few meetings this morning, including one with Jo and Brandon. I don't have time to hang here, and there isn't enough manpower for an officer patrol."

She stomped her foot. "Tommy, I'll not be run out of my place of business. I can protect myself. You made certain of that." She glared at him.

"I know you can. I'm asking you for a favor to me. I hate to have anything happen to someone who cooks these sorts of breakfast rolls and brews perfect coffee," said Tommy with a grin.

A sudden knock at the back door caused both of them to jump.

"Lily, hey, it's Renata and Ann. Why's the door locked?" Renata called.

Lily wiped her hands and moved to turn the key. Renata and Ann entered.

Ann said, "I'd like to take a couple of your rolls home to Hank if you don't mind, Lily."

"Sure. Is a dozen enough?"

"Yes, thanks."

Tommy nodded to Lily. "Hey, Ann. Can Lily spend the day at your place? I heard you were helping Jo with chores at her place. I know Lily would love to assist. She needs to close Flower for the day." He eyed Lily, hoping he wouldn't have to bring Boris into the discussion. Thankfully, she got the message.

"Yeah, um…had to call for a repair. Renata, can you go to school early, maybe to the library?"

"Yes, ma'am," she replied. "I have a big test today and wouldn't mind more review time."

"I'd love the company, Lily," Ann said. "We can catch up on the latest gossip." She placed a finger on her chin. "I did see a car parked outside. I bet whoever it was is waiting for you to open. I can go check, and maybe you can give him something to go."

"Him?"

"Yes, I've not seen him before. I thought you had a guest for a minute, but he didn't go in the front door using the keypad. It was a nice black Lexus."

Lily nodded toward Tommy. Fear crossed her eyes, and he rushed to look out front. He returned a few minutes later. "He must have seen everyone arrive and decided to come back later. Put out the sign, Lily. I can take Renata to school, and you girls can have a morning hen party."

They chuckled.

"Let me put this food away and change," Lily clapped. I get to play hooky. I'm just kidding, Renata. Hooky is wrong," she looked chastened.

Tommy patted her back and helped put away a few things. She rushed upstairs to change while Renata made a sign and, under the chief's watchful eye, taped it to the outside over the operation hours sign.

Lily locked the door and headed out back toward Ann's car.

"I'll pick you up later, Lily, and bring you home," Ann stated.

Tommy dropped Renata at the school and headed toward his office.

"Go or stay," Boris yelled, seeing the police cruiser in front of Flower B&B. He pounded the wheel. Then, another sedan passed by with two women, one staring right at him. That vehicle, following the delivery signs, turned behind the building. Swearing, he put his car into gear and drove away.

Boris took the interstate south and pulled into the 24-hour gas stop catering to truckers. He took his laptop and decided to use their Wi-Fi to plan his next steps. He wanted to see if he could help get Mikhail released. Long ago, they had set up a plan to get help if needed.

"Good morning," announced the perky waitress with a smile, batting her eyelashes. "Your car sho' is pretty. Are those Lexus as lovely inside as they look outside?"

Boris sighed. *Women were easy to manipulate. You never know when an opportunity will appear.* "Good morning to you," he said, thickening his accent. "What do you recommend for breakfast? I'm famished."

"We have the best French toast, and I can add three eggs on the side any way you want them. I prefer them sunny-side up myself." She winked at him.

"Sounds perfect. Add a cup of black coffee and a ham steak. Do you have a Wi-Fi password I can use?"

She grabbed a piece of paper from her apron pack and handed it over. "Here you go."

"Thank you. Do you live around here?"

Blush rose from her neck, visible from the low neckline of her pale blue uniform to her cheeks, and she giggled. "Sort of. I live in the town of Magnolia Bluff, just north of here. I have my whole twenty-four years."

Boris couldn't believe his luck. "That's a long time to stay in one place. I bet you know everyone. Is it true that small Texas towns have gossip trees that convey information faster than the internet?"

She nodded. "I hear it all, too. Let me get your order in. You can use your computer. If you want to know any local gossip, ask. Employed here, I get news from all over. Magnolia Bluff recently found a murdered man." She hurried away to place his order and help a customer at the counter.

After firing up his laptop and connecting, he made a list of loose ends and checked to see if Mikhail had been allowed his phone call.

CHAPTER 37

Fitting Pieces Together

An hour later, Brandon escorted Jo toward Chief Jager's conference room.

Tommy scowled, standing as they entered. Brandon sensed they were headed for a challenging, no-nonsense discussion.

Tommy stated, "It's eight o'clock on day six of the investigation, and we don't have a viable suspect who passes all the tests."

Jo brightly asked, "If JJ is no longer a suspect, I'd like our rental car and his cell phone back, please. I need to be mobile."

"Tommy," Brandon commented, "we've given you all the clues and research we've uncovered on the case. Our information was reliable enough to find Rawley's computer last night. We've explained that JJ built the beaconing software your suspect inadvertently lit up yesterday. We are closer to the truth; you have a suspect in custody. What's missing?"

Tommy growled, "Tell me about the picture of Lily and Boris you took at the restaurant but didn't bother to send to me."

Brandon looked down and shook his head. He pulled out his cell phone and showed Tommy, then Jo, the picture. "Lily and her date were having so much fun they were loud enough to be a distraction. I commented on her having a companion. Joyce twisted around to look. She turned white as a sheet and began mumbling incoherently. I followed my hunch and went over to snap a photo. It upset Lily's date, Boris. As far as I can tell, Joyce hit a mental speed bump, and she's recalling some of those lost memories. But she isn't ready to talk in a group setting. On top of that, I hated leaving her alone this morning."

Tommy pushed an FBI Wanted sheet on Vladimir Sokolov and pointed. "Do you recognize that name from the printouts we found on Rawley's printer?"

Brandon was stunned as he looked from the paper to his cell phone. Scrolling through his stored images, several minutes passed before he said, "Oh my goodness."

"Brandon, your instincts were correct; there was something wrong," confirmed Tommy. "This criminal is hunting for a computer. You interrupted his effort to pull information from Lily. What else are you not telling me?"

Jo cleared her throat and looked the chief square in the eye. "Uh…in addition to the beaconing software, JJ installed a computer virus to stop the blackmailer from using his laptop. My uh…research suggests that JJ delivered a USB drive labeled so the blackmailer would believe it contained a hundred thousand dollars in cryptocurrency. It only held the tracker computer virus."

Tommy flipped up the laptop lid atop the table. He turned it around to show the challenge screen the blackmailer would have seen.

Jo innocently shrugged. "Yes, that's something JJ would have written as a demand. Wouldn't you if you could?"

"Based on the timing of the blackmailer's email demands and the first bounce location," Brandon speculated, "we believe JJ could have confronted the blackmailer, but something else happened."

Tommy and Jo's phones pinged with incoming message alerts.

The chief read the message and saw Jo staring at the screen, too stunned to speak, but tears filled her eyes.

Tommy smiled. "Let's talk to the computer genius who just came out of his coma and wants to see his bride."

They rose to depart. Tommy locked the laptop in his private safe. Grabbing Jo's keys from the safe, he pitched them to her as they hurried toward their vehicles.

"Thank you, Tommy." Jo fidgeted with the keys.

Brandon offered, "Jo, I'll drive you to the hospital. We can get your car from impound later. I know you don't want any delays in seeing JJ."

"That would be perfect. Thanks."

Brandon caught Jo twisting her fingers in her lap during the short trip to the hospital. "It's got to be a good sign, especially if he was moved to a private room."

She placed her hands on her thighs. "I hope so. The waiting's been awful."

"Why don't you text Lily and Ann so they can get the good news flowing."

He felt her eyes on him. "I'm not sure what else to say other than he's out of ICU and awake."

"That's a great start. Since I'm driving, how about adding Joyce to the text? Tell them you're headed to the hospital and will update them soon."

Jo's fingers rapidly tapped the screen, sounding like an upbeat tap-dance jazz number. Brandon grinned. Maybe JJ could fill in some of the blanks. He heard multiple posts sent and decided Jo had included her support team. Brandon hoped JJ hadn't lost his memory like Joyce.

"Wow, I'm getting several encouraging responses. I love this town. What did Joyce do after she saw Boris's photo? Did anything click?" asked Jo.

"I didn't show it to her. She left the restaurant while I went to take the photo. Later, she was upset at her house from the experience, and I didn't want to make it worse. I'm hoping she'll remember on her own."

"That makes sense. Maybe JJ will recognize him. It's stunning that the Russian is being hunted by federal authorities. I hope Lily is safe."

Brandon pulled into the parking place next to Chief Jager and turned off the car. "Me too."

Jo led the way to the elevators, with both men following her. She pressed the desired floor, then hopped back and forth on her toes as if to hurry the ascent. The original text had indicated JJ had been moved to a private room, and the guard was stationed outside.

Jo rushed down the hallway as soon as the elevator opened. Ignoring the guard, who she decided should know her by now, she pushed open the door. Looking around, she spotted a machine beeping with the familiar line of heartbeat and oxygen levels and sighed with relief.

Sliding the updated chart into its holder by the bed, the nurse said, "Let's not overstress him. He's doing exceptionally well. We had him walking a little, and his balance has improved, but we don't want him overtired."

"I'll do better next time, ma'am," JJ said to the nurse. Oh, Jo," his voice sounded relieved. "You're here!"

Jo beamed and threw out her arms as if she would tackle JJ. At the last second, she gently enveloped him with a tearful hug. "I was so worried. You look amazing." She turned toward Tommy and Brandon. "Doesn't he look good?"

Jo was grateful that Tommy appeared pleased. Brandon grinned at her and added a thumbs-up motion. Jo slid onto the edge of the bed and held JJ's hand, his thumb brushing across hers.

"The nurse said you were walking, but how are you feeling?" Tommy asked with a concerned tone.

JJ teased, "A bit of a headache and sore ribs. Did you add something to my drinks during the housewarming party?"

Jo noticed Tommy's furrowed brow. "You know I didn't, son. Not my style."

"I was trying to gauge how much trouble I'm in with you. That poker face of yours is unreadable," JJ admitted, then chuckled.

The invisible weight in the room lifted, along with a collective sigh. Jo released the breath she'd unknowingly held. "If you're trying to joke, you're on the mend."

JJ took a sip of water from a glass Jo held out. "Tommy, I owe you an apology. I promised to let you handle the blackmailer, yet when I deciphered the email, I realized the time was ticking to meet the deadline he'd imposed. I intended to alert you when the delivery occurred." He took another sip of water from the hospital cup. "I built a program to gain his location and provided that in the drop-off, rather than the crypto demanded. I planned to spring on him when the signal alerted us to where he was." He focused on Tommy. "I'm not certain what occurred next. I'm not quite up to what day it is today. The doctor said that's normal because the drugs used to reduce brain swelling haven't washed completely out of my system."

Jo watched Tommy's frown deepen. She knew Joyce's memory was gone but recognized he wanted the truth.

Tommy shifted his stance. He folded his arms across his chest, then leveled his gaze on JJ as he evenly said, "We found you unconscious next to Rawley's body. The evidence suggested you were his killer."

JJ briefly closed his eyes. "He's dead?"

"Yep. Both of you had bruises suggesting a fight or a beating," Tommy continued. "Your wife, with Brandon's help, gathered clues to change that opinion. Your computer virus seized Rawley's computer. Somehow Jo learned the coordinates so we could find it. We located the computer and have a suspect in custody."

JJ grinned. "Great, it worked." He squeezed Jo's hand, and she felt the silent exchange that she'd done the right thing.

"Joyce was also found at the scene," Jo added. "Her memory is locked away because of what she must have seen. She wasn't physically injured, but she thought you were dead."

JJ's eyes widened, and his jaw clenched. "That's awful."

"She may have seen something. Brandon's been working with me while trying to help her. She lost her voice for a while, but it returned."

Tommy asked, "What else can you tell us? Can you walk it back to when we spoke early Monday morning?"

JJ nodded. "Not long after you left, our email box was inundated with spam, which made tracing the origination point nearly impossible. The messaging was clear on crypto demands and where to deliver them—including an unrealistic deadline. I assembled the program and set up some triggers to monitor, which I planned to use later."

Jo watched as he swallowed and sipped the water again, licking his lips. "Do you need to rest, honey?" Jo asked.

He shook his head. "After I made the drop in the donation box, he got away. I waited for him to install the USB and the beacon to begin. I figured it would be a while, so I decided to call you. I remember scrolling to your number when my phone app notified me the signal was operational. The GPS coordinates came through. I ended up at a house on Hickory Street." JJ tilted his head and squinted, then ran his hand over his face. "Yeah. I parked in the driveway. The door was open. I walked in and heard him cussing a blue streak. I entered the dining room as he slammed the cover on his PC, shutting it down." JJ took another drink. "I admit I was mad, Tommy. I pulled him up by his armpits, ready to clock him. I thought he would say something, maybe beg, when his eyes appeared terrified by something behind me. I was so focused that I didn't hear anything. I spun around to see them. There were two." Jo felt him squeeze her hand.

He breathed and continued, "You can't mistake the whirling sound of nunchaku. I turned in time to catch one on the side of my head. The guy was good. He hit three more times in rapid succession before I went down." JJ stared off as if trying to see the picture replaying. "I need to add that attack to my daily workout."

"If I show you some photos," Tommy asked, "could you identify the men?"

"I think so," JJ said. "But if it's them, I want a rematch."

Jo's entire body was filled with anger and fear. She stormed, "What? This wasn't friendly combat. You're lucky to be alive, JJ."

Tommy smirked. "I think you have the answer on that topic. Thanks, Jo."

The chief displayed the photo taken when Reece booked the guy from the hotel and the one Brandon captured at the restaurant.

JJ studied them both. "Yes, that's them."

Jo sensed Tommy was satisfied.

"Let me call the station and see if he's answering questions," said Tommy. "He claimed to be Lithuanian. Based on the older man Boris, aka Vladimir's rap sheet, I'm voting he's Russian. We'll do something more formal once you're out of here."

Tommy dialed the station but received no answer. He tried two other numbers; they both went to voice mail. He groaned, "Brother, I leave the station on business, and no one's around to answer the phone. It'll have to wait until…"

Tommy's phone rang.

CHAPTER 38

Time to Hit Back

Chief Tommy Jager answered the call, snarling, "Where were you? I've called all three numbers…No…What the hell was t he senator doing at the station? No one stopped them…Where's Reece? Well, don't tell him…Why did you let him call anyone before I interviewed him? We have twenty hours before we need to offer that…The guy did what? Did you call the paramedics? I'll make that call and be there as soon as possible…

Tommy issued a long-suffering sigh. "Yes, send a still photo from the camera footage in the office and then issue an all-points bulletin for the apprehension and detention of both men…Hell, yes, armed and dangerous."

Tommy disconnected and turned to find three pairs of eyes staring at him. "That's just fine as a frog's hair. Someone hit the station, freed the prisoner, and demanded the laptop. The good news is they knocked out the senator, which will keep him out of my hair until I figure out his role in this mess."

JJ tried to get up, but Jo pressed him back onto the pillow. "Where do you think you're going?"

"Nowhere. My head still hurts when I move too fast. Tommy, the computer virus I built is unbreakable. They think the material on the laptop is critical, or they wouldn't risk hitting a police station. I bet they're coders and know getting the virus's author is their only option for access to the machine."

Tommy displayed an uncharacteristic grin. "I like it when criminals provide an idea for their capture. If you're right, JJ, they'll strike again. We need to plan ahead of them." He moved closer to JJ and looked him over. "Keep me posted on the doctor's estimated discharge date."

"I'm expecting two days at the most," JJ replied, "though they say I may need additional physical therapy."

Tommy tapped his fingers against his thigh. "Jo, stay close to JJ so you both are protected by my deputy. If you must go home, make sure someone is there. I can call Hank and Ann if you wish. Lily is with them today and would love to hear about JJ's improvements." Tommy narrowed his eyes at them both. "No more cowboy stunts, young man. We will plan together if you're involved."

JJ nodded sheepishly.

"Brandon," he continued, "stay close to Joyce. Let me know if she regains more of her memory. Remain vigilant until we find and detain these guys for questioning."

Tommy left them, giving orders to the deputy posted outside the room.

"Nurse, do you have another room to move Mr. Rodreguiz into?"

She consulted her monitor and nodded. "I have one on the other side of this floor."

"He needs to be moved immediately. Put him under an alias. Keep it classified. If anyone inquires, call me."

The nurse paled, with eyes blinking her alarm.

"No need to worry. My deputy is on duty. I'll ask him to come help."

She called one of the interns, then nodded to Tommy.

Tommy sent a text to his deputy as he headed to his cruiser. He muttered, "I've got a few details to attend to."

CHAPTER 39

Winning Arguments

Jo stood and paced after the chief left. She resumed her seat on the bed next to JJ and questioned, "Do you think I should ask the nurse when the doctor will arrive? I'd like to understand your status."

"I'll head down and get some coffee," Brandon offered. "I can let the nurse know if you want."

"Thanks," Jo said with a grin.

"Do you want me to bring you anything?"

"No thanks." She raised her hand, which held JJ's. "I've got everything I want right here."

Brandon chuckled on his way out.

JJ reached up and turned her face toward him, his fingers warm on her chin. With a mischievous expression, raising his eyebrows, he seductively whispered, "Sweetheart, did you send him on an errand so you could take liberties with me?"

Jo laughed. "The coma hasn't diminished your friskiness. We'll get a ruling from the doctor before I take you home."

JJ's expression sobered. "Babe, I'm sorry I messed everything up this week. You look like you haven't slept well. You did great connecting with Brayson. I'm glad he found my files and directions."

"It wasn't your fault. Brayson has been our champion through all of this. He accessed your computer and found the virus's beaconing software. We've recreated everything you told Tommy. He kept me centered. I asked him not to tell your folks for the time being. Your doctor has contacted your regular doctor regarding your progress here."

"Good. No need to worry the families or have them show up trying to help." JJ rubbed his thumb across the top of her hand.

"I agree. It wasn't easy keeping Brayson from hopping on a plane." Apprehension filled her mind. "Brandon helped me access the crime scene. We assembled additional pieces of evidence for Tommy. We argued when he wouldn't release your phone or the rental car, insisting it was evidence."

"That was nice of Brandon to drive you around, especially if Joyce wasn't feeling one hundred percent. I'm glad she wasn't attacked, too," he said, gently rubbing his ribs.

"Brandon's investigative experience helped me." Her lips trembled. "I worry you'll want to sell our place when the culprits are in custody. Ann and Hank have been checking on me. They are helping with the watering. I'm ready for you to come home."

"Me too."

Jo lamented, "Vladimir, or Boris, took Lily on a date and then interrogated her about people in Magnolia Bluff. The murder was in the paper, but your name wasn't mentioned. Joyce's memories may be returning from seeing Boris with Lily at dinner. She was so upset she left. You've always said bad guys don't give up easily. I think this is one of those people."

JJ nodded. "You're probably right, honey. If it were to leak that a computer geek, a person of interest in the murder, is hospitalized, they might attempt to question me. After all, if they were bold enough to hit a police station, a hospital would be easier."

Jo's heart dropped to her stomach. "No! You won't be bait for these killers. Don't do that to me, honey."

"I don't want that scum to threaten Lily or to find Joyce. Who knows what they'll do if they think Joyce is a witness? I don't want anyone bothering Lily. When our friends need help, we may not have a choice."

Anger welled inside her, but she kept quiet, biting her lip.

"I'm not a hundred percent, but I will try if needed. I want your support if it comes to that. You have the heart of a lioness. Even Tommy knows you're formidable."

Jo wiped her tears and slapped her hand on her thigh. "Grr. I hate arguing with you when you're right."

The door swooshed open; the doctor entered. "Good, I'm glad you're here, Mrs. Rodreguiz. Your husband is doing better…"

"Doc, I'm right here." JJ pointed a thumb at his chest.

Appearing a bit flustered, the doctor chuckled. "Sorry, Mr. Rodreguiz." He flipped up a page on the chart. "Your tests came back improved. I prefer you remain here for a couple of days to monitor. I've scheduled three physical therapy sessions today and four tomorrow. Your recovery will be rapid due to your age and muscle tone."

Jo felt giddy. "I can take my husband home in a couple of days?"

The doctor nodded. "Yes, unless something unexpected occurs. The therapy should help him regain some strength quickly. We can run tests if needed."

She leaned in and gave JJ a full kiss, lasting a few heartbeats.

The doctor cleared his throat.

JJ grinned. "And no restrictions?"

The doctor laughed. "I doubt you'd abide by them anyway." He closed the chart. "I'll be back in the morning unless something changes."

When the doctor left, JJ took her in his arms and murmured into her ear, "I can't wait to get you home."

She hugged him back and jumped off the bed. "I agree. I'm going to find Brandon and get the rental car. I'll return later, honey. Please don't make any plans to be bait until WE can speak with Tommy. I'll update Brayson. Love you." She leaned in for one last smooch before dancing out the door. She heard his familiar wolf whistle as she turned right toward the elevators.

Brandon met Jo outside the main entrance. She jumped in his truck, tightened her seat belt, and waited, unable to stop smiling. She asked, "Have you thought about putting in an escalator so folks can get in here gracefully?"

Brandon chuckled. "Guys appreciate high-riding trucks. You wouldn't understand."

Jo smirked and remarked with her best Texas accent, "I get it. It's a Texas thang."

He laughed, set the GPS toward the impound yard, and asked, "Jo, can I get a favor? Joyce still has memory issues. She redoubled her efforts last night by doodling on her notebook pad. With the rap sheet on Vladimir, I'd like to swing by and get Joyce. Jason is at school, and then he has practice. With the escape of these killers, I don't want her alone, even with Max for protection."

"That's a great idea. I'd like to see her. Tommy told you to keep her close. I wouldn't tell her about the stuff at the police station."

"Agreed." A few minutes later, Brandon pulled the vehicle into Joyce's driveway. "Hey, do you want to come along, or will the missing escalator be a problem again?"

Jo chuckled. "I can handle it. I was kidding."

Brandon rushed to open the passenger side for her, and she hopped to the ground. They headed toward the main entry, where Brandon used his key.

He hollered, "Hi, I'm back. Who wants to go for a ride?"

Max galloped out, followed closely by Joyce, holding her doodle pad and pencil. She rushed to Jo and hugged her. "I'm so glad you're here. How's JJ doing?"

"We're back from the hospital. He is awake, alert, and negotiating to come home. The doctor said perhaps in a couple of days. Brandon is taking me to the impound lot behind Ciara Doyle's garage. My rental car is being released."

"I'm so glad he's recovering," Joyce said with a reticent smile.

Brandon patted Max on the head. "I thought we'd grab you to go along and gab with Jo to get caught up. We can go for ice cream or something else after. Whatever you want."

He noticed Joyce's eyes looking fearful.

"I don't think I'd be much company," replied Joyce. "Why don't you drop Jo off and come back? I'll fix you a bowl of ice cream. I made cookies earlier."

Brandon followed Jo's eyes to the scribbles on the notepad.

"After I get the car, I plan to return to the hospital." Jo patted her friend on the arm. "Join me. JJ is awake and cracking jokes. Seeing you would brighten his afternoon. Please?"

Brandon frowned at Jo and noticed Joyce staring at her feet. Jo pointed two fingers toward her eyes, then the notepad. She mouthed *JJ*. Brandon decided her idea had merit.

"Of course," he said. "We'd love to stop by and see him, right, hon?" Brandon told Max, "Buddy, I'd bring you too, but they're fussy about hound dogs in the hospital. We won't be gone but a few minutes. You take over."

Joyce appeared uneasy but acquiesced. They piled into the truck. As he backed out onto the street, Brandon saw in his rearview mirror a black SUV slowly pull up and park.

He abruptly stopped the car and hurried back to the house. Unlocking the door, he hollered, "Max, come on, boy. You can ride with us." The animal scampered out as Jo opened the back door of the vehicle. Brandon returned to the driver's seat. Max graced his right ear with grateful kisses as they all chuckled.

Brandon checked the rearview mirror, feeling uneasy, then shrugged. "I couldn't leave him alone. I like this dog."

CHAPTER 40

The Doctor's In

Brandon parked the truck and snapped on Max's leash. "Ladies, I'll bring Max into the hospital as my service dog. Back me up if I get challenged, okay?"

Jo nodded her agreement. Joyce stayed at his side as if psyching herself up, chewing on the side of one nail. They arrived at the room after two challenges on the dog. He was reminded to use the service dog's halter collar.

The deputy greeted them. "Y'all go on in. Miss Joyce, it's nice to see you."

Joyce looked at the deputy and murmured, "Thanks," yet she remained as if her feet were nailed to the floor.

Brandon, holding Max close, was concerned.

Jo slid her arm through Joyce's. "Thank you for coming. I know he's going to enjoy seeing you."

Joyce remained anchored to the spot.

"Did I ever tell you how JJ helped me overcome my fears? One day, I wigged out in front of the people I worked with, then ran and hid. JJ found me and convinced me I needed to face my fears. That was the hardest thing to do. His confidence in me made all the difference. It's time for you to face your fears. I'm right here, and Brandon is here to support you." She gently tugged Joyce's arm, and they eased through the door and into the room.

JJ beamed. "Wow, it's great to have this attention. I just returned from one of my PT sessions. Grueling."

Jo leaned in and kissed him. "You're looking better."

Max placed his front paws on the bed, stretching his neck for petting. JJ laughed at the antics and ruffled his ears. "You better get down. The nurse would be annoyed if she saw you."

Brandon noticed Joyce's pallor and trembling hands.

"Brandon, good to see you. Joyce, you're a pleasant surprise. How are you feeling?"

Her eyes flickered when JJ said her name. She glanced toward him, her lips quivering. "JJ, you're alive." She closed her eyes for a moment, then gently shook her head. "When I saw Rawley, then you, lying there so still…I got scared." Her breathing increased. Brandon feared she'd hyperventilate, so he moved closer and rubbed her back.

She continued in a staccato voice, "It was so quiet until… I looked around at a sound from the hallway. A man's image appeared in the mirror for a second. I…uh, reached for my phone to call the police." She covered her face with one hand. "My hands were shaking as I dialed. I backed up to leave, terrified I would see the face again." She looked toward Brandon. "The man was in the restaurant with Lily. I had to leave." Her eyes met JJ's. "I don't know what happened before I was in an ambulance. Tommy was there. A gurney had a sheet over someone. I thought it was you. I worried about how to tell Jo." Her hands flew to her face as she started to sob.

JJ reached out, his fingers brushing her arm. "I'm all right, Joyce. Alive because of you, I suspect. Thank you."

Brandon was stunned. He reached his arm around her shoulders, pulling her close. "Your memory is back. It'll all be okay. I'll be with you when you tell Tommy. I won't let anything happen to you."

Tear-filled eyes looked at Jo. "Thank you for convincing me to face my fears."

The two women hugged and parted, sharing a smile. Jo snuggled up next to JJ.

Brandon grinned at the exchanged looks as Jo resettled JJ's pillows. Brandon guided Joyce to a side chair. Max followed, laying his head on her lap.

"Well done, Joyce. I'll call Tommy and let him know what you recall."

She nodded with a weak smile.

CHAPTER 41

Set the Trap

Tommy parked his cruiser and hurried into the station. "Where are we? Is everyone all right?"

Reece turned to face the chief and shifted his cigar to the left side. "The medics took the senator to the hospital. His aide followed in the limo. One deputy got treated, but he's back at it." He pointed to the man at the corner desk wearing a bandage on his face. "I returned as soon as I heard."

Tommy struggled to contain his annoyance. "What the hell was David doing here? I didn't invite him. On the phone, the deputy said the senator demanded access to information on the blackmailer's PC." Laser-focused on Reece's eyes, Tommy leaned down so there would be no mistaking his point. "How did he know it was here, Reece?"

Reece nervously rolled the cigar around his mouth, trying not to break eye contact. "Uh, you know how well plugged in that guy is. He talks to everyone about votes while his aide takes notes to use later. The gossip mill must be in high gear for him to have learned you received it yesterday."

Tommy knew the man was waffling. Most times, Reece was an average detective, but this time, he may have stepped over the line. "It's a shame you removed the laptop from my safe. It was infected with an unbreakable virus." He rubbed his chin with his fingertips, deep in thought. "Let's say I'm the only one who can open the machine and disable the virus. Old Vlad will have to talk to me about access. Let's see how fast the gossipers can share this news."

"What?" Reece sputtered, "You know how to get into it?"

Tommy continued with a wry smile. He wanted Reece to come clean. "We each have secrets, I guess." He slapped Reece on the back. "The suspect can't access it without me. There is a fortune in blackmail information on that PC that can't be exposed without my help, except for maybe JJ." Tommy shifted and turned toward his office. "Did you do an all-points bulletin to the regular channels? I hope you didn't put out too much information. I don't want us to look like clowns."

Reece straightened. "I took care of the APB."

Tommy shot him a dejected look.

Reece missed the subtleties.

Tommy's phone vibrated. He pulled it from his shirt pocket. "This is Chief Jager…Understood. I'll head right over…Right. Thanks." Tommy returned his phone to his pocket and repositioned his hat as he turned.

"Where do I need to focus my efforts?" Reece asked.

Tommy sarcastically replied, "Why don't you see how David is doing and keep him informed?"

Tommy pulled his cruiser to the curb just past the tiny structure of a 1950s circa two-bedroom house. The emergency call took him to a road he rarely traveled. The information he received indicated the home was deeded to the original owner. EMT personnel dashed between their vehicle and the little white house with faded blue trim. Tommy ducked as he stepped inside in time to watch them place a woman on their gurney. Off to the side, an older man with white hair, a wrinkled shirt, and rumbled pants stared silently at the activity.

Tommy walked to the man. "You the one who found her?"

The man nodded. When he looked at Tommy, his eyes were full of unshed tears. "Yep, she missed her shift at the truck stop. That's not like Stacie. When my best waitress doesn't check in, I get worried."

Tommy nodded and moved to the paramedic. "Can I ask her some questions before you take her?"

"I figured you'd want to talk to her," the woman replied. "She's had some pain meds but should still be coherent. We must leave within the next five minutes, so get to it, Chief."

Tommy hurried to the patient's side. "Stacie, who did this?"

"A man," she mumbled with tears winding down her cheeks toward her ears as she lay on her back.

"Did he give a name?" Tommy reached for his phone and brought up a photo. "Did he look like this?"

She squinted to study the photo. With pursed lips, she replied weakly, "That's him. Smooth talker. Russian accent. He claimed he was scouting a movie location. I brought him here. I told him it was quaint but so pretty. He asked endless questions about the newspaper article on the murder." She choked a bit and winced. "He demanded information on some computer. I told him *no comprendo*. He got mad and demanded to know who in town could help. I said the only computer guru I knew was JJ Rodreguiz, but he was hospitalized this week. I told him I attended their housewarming party, where we boogied all night. He wanted a map. I said no. Then he started beating me with sticks with a chain between."

Tommy took a deep breath and nodded to the paramedic. They needed to leave. He patted Stacie's arm. "We'll find him. Thank you."

Tommy returned to the older man. "A shame she was so trusting."

He responded, "Young folks trust easily and rarely see the risks. It's why she's such a good waitress. She makes good money serving truck drivers and travelers. People like having a friendly person to visit with between destinations."

"I know she's grateful you checked. Can you lock up her house and alert her folks?"

"Yes. It's my rental house." His eyes filled with water as he looked up. "She's my daughter, Chief."

CHAPTER 42

Roundup

Tommy's phone vibrated, indicating someone needed him. He pulled it from his pocket, studied the name for a heartbeat, and then answered, "Tommy, here. Whatcha got?"

His deputy reported, "Chief, we've got a situation at the hospital. The senator woke. He's making life miserable for everyone. He's demanding police protection. I'm the only one around. I can't cover Rodreguiz and the senator unless we put them in the same room. The senator is demanding a private room."

Tommy smirked. "I told Reece to talk to the senator. When he gets there, have him do guard duty for David. I need you back here anyway because Rodreguiz is going home today."

The deputy blew out a breath that sounded like relief. "Thanks for getting me out of here."

"Don't tell anyone you're leaving," the chief added.

After he disconnected, he phoned Jo. When she answered, he said, "Hey, this is Tommy. How soon can you get JJ out and home?"

"I think you misunderstood," Jo stated. "The doctor said he was doing great but needed to remain for observation and physical therapy until the day after tomorrow. Why do you want him out now? He changed rooms as you requested."

"I want him home as soon as possible, but I need everyone to believe he's still in the hospital. Ask the staff to move him quietly using an ambulance. After he is home, arrange to have the PT staff come there. I can allocate funds to cover the costs."

With a tone of dismay, Jo asked, "What's wrong? Is he in danger from the Russian madman?"

"I don't know," Tommy confessed, "but I'd like to protect him. He is a likely target because he can identify the killer. My best defense is to keep him hidden until I nail this guy."

Jo succinctly stated, "*Our* best defense, Tommy. I'm in this with you. We could let some details slip out so Vladimir knows where to find JJ."

"The guy knows where to find him…in the hospital. I suspect the jerk is closing in," admitted Tommy.

Jo, half chuckling, squeaked, "JJ will love part of this takedown. I'll call Brandon to help. I believe he's got good news for you."

"Thanks for reminding me. I need to talk to him. Let me know when you get JJ home."

Reece frowned and nearly spat out his cigar. "Deputy, what did you say? It sounded like you want me to guard the senator. I'm a detective, not a nursemaid."

The man yawned. "I'm relaying the chief's message. Call him if you're unhappy with the assignment."

Reece grumbled, kicking his feet and scuffing the floor as he walked to the senator's room. He arrived in time to hear the nurse yell, "I'm not the fresh food section for squeezing, so keep your hands off my butt, mister."

Reece pushed open the door.

The patient was startled at the intrusion until he recognized Reece. "Oh, it's you. Am I getting police protection while I'm here?"

Reece half-smiled an apology to the angry-looking nurse, who stomped out of the room. "You did it anyway? I told you not to barge into the office demanding the laptop to erase your involvement, but you did anyway. I'm your assigned police protection. Happy now?"

David sputtered, "What? If you're stuck at the hospital, how can I stay current on Magnolia Bluff events?" He sucked the straw of the water container on the side table. "Did they catch the stick-wielding maniac?"

"No. He sprang his accomplice. Both are at large with the laptop."

The senator frantically waved his hands. "We've got to get it back. Let me get dressed. I'll call my aide to bring the car and—"

"Your aide isn't here. Without formal discharge papers, you aren't going anywhere. Besides, all your items are locked in the hospital safe. They were afraid your valuable possessions might go missing. Unless you want to head out in a hospital gown with your butt showing, you'll have to wait."

The senator paled, closed his eyes, and mumbled, "They called next of kin. I bet my wife told them to do that. She's probably still laughing." He turned toward Reece. "You'd better come up with something if you still want that favor from me. I want that machine so I can erase—"

Tired, Reece barked, "You can't do a darn thing with it unless you have the passphrase to de-activate the virus. Tommy has the other piece to the puzzle. Getting it won't cure your problem. This is why you should have let me work it."

Jo opened the room door to stick her head in and confirmed, "Oh, Mr. Sovern, good. They told me I'd find you here. Where's the deputy who was guarding my husband? His new room is close to here; perhaps he's lost."

Reece slowly replied, "He was pulled off. I'm the only one here. I'm assigned to the senator." He thrust his thumb behind him.

The senator brightened. "Reece, if there's no one else on duty, let me suggest you sit in the hallway to watch both doors. The little lady and the senator each get protection. You'll be doing us a favor."

Jo smiled prettily and exclaimed, "Why, thank you. I'm sorry I didn't recognize you without your clothes."

A frown quickly replaced David's smile. "We may have gotten off on the wrong foot, ma'am."

Suppressing his smirk, Reece escorted Jo to the hall. Then sat on the chair between the rooms.

CHAPTER 43

Ready to Strike

Hospitals were not Jo's favorite places, especially this one. Jo studied her husband's face as he slept. The drone from the monitoring equipment created a weird alien-like environment. JJ's random hand and arm movements kept Jo seated at a safe distance.

Jo's phone rang a favorite song. She answered, "Brayson, it's late for you. What's up?"

"I'm seeing a black SUV at the gate to your house."

Jo furrowed her brow. "How do you know that?"

"From the video feeds JJ installed. I'm watching the telemetry coming in on his laptop. I established a watcher program to alert me if anything came into view unannounced. The app to open the gate didn't sound."

"Brayson, it might be the same vehicle used by the suspect Vladimir, who took Lily out on a date. It shadowed us at Joyce's when we went to the hospital. Are Lily and Ann still there at our house?"

"No, they left a few hours ago. They did set the alarm. The house is quiet. The electronic gate is closed…Wait a minute. The vehicle is turning around to leave." He exhaled. "No forced entry. Your house is secure."

Jo breathed a sigh of relief.

"I've spoken with the doctor. He agreed to let JJ go home early in the morning. Tommy wants us out of the hospital as soon as possible. The Russian has us on his radar."

"Jo, you said Vladimir knows JJ is at the hospital. If that SUV is his, it means he knows where you live. Do you still have police protection at the hospital?"

Jo rolled her eyes as she thought of Reece as protection. "I guess you could say yes. I'd better go out in the hall to wake him up. It's Detective Reece."

"You mean the guy who can't get the correct coffee and donut order?" Brayson pressed. "Did you make Tommy mad again?"

Jo snorted, then sniffled, "Please don't yell at me. I'm doing the best I can."

"Jo, I'm sorry, I didn't mean to fuss at you. It's tough to sit so far away and feel unable to help. I know it's worse for you."

Jo drew a ragged breath. "You've assisted me this far. We can't quit now. Thank you for the monitoring. It makes us better prepared. I'll let Tommy know about the prowling SUV."

Senator David slipped from bed and peeked out the door to check on Reece. The detective was slumped in the semi-comfortable chair, softly snoring. The senator frowned and padded barefoot to the nurse's station while holding the back of his gown to keep his backside covered. The duty nurse appeared dismayed when she realized he was at the counter.

He motioned for with his index finger pressed to his lips. He whispered, "I need to get to my clothes and retrieve some items you have locked up. They should not be out of my possession."

The nurse eyed him suspiciously.

"As a legislative representative to the voters of this state," he added, "I'm obligated to keep them under my control and confidential. Please show me where my belongings are."

The nurse went to a door behind her and returned a few minutes later with a bag containing his possessions. He rifled through the bag and nearly sighed in delight as his fingers grasped the all-important thumb drive. He turned to collide face-to-face with Reece.

Reece smiled and reported, "To be a gunnery sergeant, one must be a light sleeper and curious about what everyone is doing. Those traits have helped get me to a detective level. Thanks to your sleepwalking, I'm curious about the USB drive you're holding onto for dear life, with your naked butt hanging out."

The senator looked at the floor.

"We should have found a USB drive along with Rawley's PC at the murder scene," Reece continued, "but we didn't. We finally located the laptop and one suspect, but not the drive. Tell me about the drive in your hand and how you came by it. It's not a common item most people carry."

CHAPTER 44

Reconnaissance, Then Attack

Brandon parked his truck in the driveway and took Joyce's hand. "Honey, you haven't said anything on our drive home. What's going on in that pretty head of yours?"

He noticed her eyes welling with tears. "I'm a mess. First, I was terrified I'd never remember. Now I'm scared, stupid. I'll never forget the murder scene. I know I'm supposed to talk to Tommy and tell him everything. I don't—"

Brandon's phone rang. He accepted the call. "Hi, Chief. Joyce and I were talking about you…Yes, she's recovered her memory. The scene's reality is more than she bargained for…No, I'm not sure that's a good idea. I'm not a shrink, but I know distress when I see it. She needs some time…That's a good idea. You said his name is Dr. Michael Kurelek? I'll ask her to call him tomorrow …I agree her testimony is important, but she needs to feel confident answering those questions without mental anguish…Oh, he's helped on other cases. Good to know…You're right. You shouldn't need her identification until after he's apprehended… Thanks for understanding, Tommy…Talk later."

Max, anxious to get out and play with Brandon, delivered a big, wet, sloppy lick that drenched his ear. Brandon turned to face the pup and spotted the same SUV approaching in the rearview mirror.

His heart raced, and panic spread as he was consumed by the need to protect his family.

Jason bounded out the front door and leaned on the passenger side. "Are you going to sit in the truck all night, or are we having supper?"

Brandon commented through the open window. "Jason, hop in. We're eating out."

"I'm not up to visiting with anyone else or going out," Joyce protested.

Brandon patted her hand. "That SUV at the driveway's edge is the one from before. I don't want to risk a confrontation. Jason, come on. Drive-through dinner tonight."

Joyce gripped his hand tight as Jason entered the truck.

Tommy answered his mobile phone, feeling lucky. "Hi, Jo. You've arrived home already?"

"The doctor said tomorrow," she replied, "even after I explained how important it was to you. But I've got a new problem. JJ's cameras picked up a black SUV at the gate of my house. The gate stopped him because he had no code. At least he didn't climb over. With no cars in front or the lights on, he must have thought no one was home. The video cameras showed the car leaving minutes later."

Tommy huffed. "Vladimir learned JJ's whereabouts from a new victim. Jo, stay alert. Let Reece know I'll be there as soon as I can."

Jo complained, "Why did you pull the deputy out and put Reece in? I don't feel as safe, though JJ says it'll be all right."

"Reece's military background is his redeeming quality. He's good in a fight. And he owes these suspects."

CHAPTER 45

Prep Time

Lily grinned at the incoming caller's picture and tapped Ann on the shoulder. "Hi, Jo. How's JJ? Is he ready to come home? I know you can't wait. I'm putting you on speaker so Hank and Ann can hear."

"I'm glad you're together. We'll be home tomorrow morning."

They all cheered.

"Good news," confirmed Lily.

Jo chuckled, "The doctor granted an early release because he's doing so well. We figured the physical therapists could come to the house. Lily, are the girls there, too?"

"Yes. We've had a great day so far. We went to your house to tidy up and water the plants. Boy, that fertilizer you're using is working. I bet you get some giant blooms soon," Promised Lily. "I'm worried about Flower, but no guests are checking in for another week. A few days of missed meals isn't awful. I promised Tommy I would stick with Ann and Hank until he said I could return home. We decided to help, but Hank wanted to replace the whiskey he'd left at your house since we drank it. When we arrived, I told Ann I'd help clean her place too. We've been laughing in between working most of the day. Almost like a mini-vacation for me."

Jo laughed. "I'm glad you're having fun. It sounds like I need more tutoring on cleaning rituals in Texas." She paused for a long minute.

Lily raised an eyebrow at Ann and pursed her lips.

Jo continued in a strained tone, "You stay there and enjoy. I'll call you when we're on the way home."

Lily frowned. "Sweetie, is something going on? Tommy had me leave my home, and you're checking on my whereabouts, sounding nervous as a cat waiting for someone to attack her kittens."

Jo's voice broke as she said, "Boy, even over the phone, you know me too well, Lily."

"Then just tell me, please."

Jo sighed, "You're a target. JJ's a target. Joyce is a target. And maybe me, too. I have police protection here at the hospital for us. Tommy is hunting for the Russian who hurt someone else, trying to locate JJ. I want everyone safe. We think he was at the house after you left to return to Ann's because our security cameras picked up the image of the SUV, but the padlocked gate stopped him. Thank heavens for whiskey. I'll call when we are headed home."

Hank asked, "Does this maniac know we have Lily?"

"I don't know how that would be possible, Hank," said Jo. "If you see a black SUV, stay inside with the door barred and call the chief."

Lily's skin crawled with goosebumps. "Don't you worry, hon. We're packing. He'll get more than expected if he shows at Hank and Ann's."

"Keep the girls close until Tommy says it's safe," Jo added.

"Don't you worry none. We'll keep everyone safe until this Russian tornado is captured."

Visions of Wealth

Vladimir wanted to leave this room and solve his problem. "We went to the address the girl provided. It is remote, but getting through the gate without understanding the security is too dangerous."

Mikhail stared intently at the computer screen and commented, "This program is a work of art. It's resisted everything I've thrown at it. It seems to know where I will poke it next. It contains a shimmering quality I've never seen. It's almost alive."

Vlad repeatedly turned the USB drive, trying to decide the best next step. His annoyance was rising. He wanted the payday included inside this device. "Great, you're fascinated but can't break it." He rubbed his fist against his mouth. "If the geek who built this virus is clever enough to stump you, we need it for our cyber-attacks. We'll make a fortune doing ransomware using this unbreakable virus."

Mikhail turned his head. "Vlad, I'm not sure how good this will be if we can't disinfect the machines to receive the payment. We know how to trick people into loading it on their machines, but without an antidote, we won't get any referrals or repeat business. We must be able to—"

Vlad waved his hand and interrupted, "All evidence points to the computer geek being our solution. We know he's in the hospital. We explain things to him until he gives us the source code. I want the magic needed to disinfect the poisoned machines. We get him, the blackmailer's list of victims, and a new source of revenue." He looked at the vision of Nirvana and said, "Just think of all the ways we can leverage a computer virus; no one can break us. We get millions being the fixers. No one needs to know we are the infectors, too."

Mikhail pushed out his lower lip and nodded. "We demand cryptocurrency to unlock target machines and move on to the next institution that can't afford to be held hostage. As good as this virus is, we won't download sensitive data from their machines and spend months selling it. We lock it up. I like your vision of Easy Street."

Tired of the prattle, Vlad stood. He placed the drive into his jeans pocket. "The computer won't heal itself. We're heading to the hospital. You can squeeze the geek for answers."

Reece smirked as he found Tommy's number and pressed to connect.

"Reece, what's up?"

Feeling smug about the catch, Reece bragged, "You remember the USB we couldn't find at Rawley's? I just confiscated one from Senator David. He admitted to getting it from Rawley." Reece confidently replaced the unlit cigar into the almost joey-like pouch of his face.

Tommy countered, "Nice work, Reece. Do you know what's on it? Is it the one JJ put into the donation box for the blackmailer to retrieve? Is this evidence or the senator's private property? There are a few gaps in our information."

Reece crumpled his face, annoyed at the lack of admiration from his boss. He rolled the cigar to the non-talking side of his face and grunted, "Chief, I don't know what's on it. The senator risked his modesty in a hospital gown to get it back from the nurse's station, which I captured in a photo on my phone. Then he clammed up like a perp under a bright light when I asked for details on the content. He wouldn't deny knowing we were looking for a missing USB from Rawley's place. It's gotta mean it has some value. What do you want me to do with the device?"

"I'll admit it's interesting, but not a crime to have a USB drive. Take it to JJ and ask him to see what's on it. The senator will explain from behind bars for decades if it's the one with the virus. Anything else on it is technically private property. Are there any labels on the outside suggesting confidential materials for government use only?"

"Nope, nothing on it other than the manufacturer's logo."

"Give it to JJ; make him sign for it. I'm headed in your direction soon. Oops, I have an incoming call I need to take. See you in a while." Tommy disconnected.

Reece grumbled, "I was hero material until he started asking me questions." After a heavy sigh, like a balloon deflating, he mumbled, "At least it is a short walk to turn this over to JJ." He searched a couple of pockets in his jacket until he found the needed pad. "Good, I had the forms on me." He rolled his eyes toward the ceiling. "Maybe something interesting is on this thing." Then he laughed. "I wonder if David will pay for my photo?"

CHAPTER 47

Needing Help

Feeling oddly distracted by the annoying Reece, Chief Jager gruffly answered the call. "What is it, Brandon?"

Brandon politely replied, "Sounds like I interrupted you, Tommy."

Tommy inhaled and let it out slowly. "Nothing's going well. What can I do for you?"

"I'm with Joyce, Jason, and Max on the way to a fast-food spot, trying to lose the black SUV. It pulled up at Joyce's place, and I decided we needed to keep moving. I think he decided not to follow or turned in a different direction. It's twice that vehicle has been there. I don't think it's safe for Joyce or Jason to be alone at home."

Tommy ruffled his hair, exasperated. "Sorry, this Russian is making life a mess. Everything and everyone involved in this murder is either hiding from this guy, or trying to find him." He sighed, running through the list of possibilities in his mind.

"I can keep my family mobile and safe, but they'll need some rest, especially Joyce. Where do you want us? And will you need my support?"

Tommy overheard Joyce say, "Brandon, I'm okay. As long as you are close, I know we're safe."

"Joyce sounds good, at least for the moment, Brandon. Call Jo. See if she minds if you bunk at her place. She has security in place and will arrive in the morning with JJ. The SUV was there but left without a way through the gate. Boris, or Vladimir, is looking for people and coming up empty. I'd like to know if all y'all are safe. He's becoming more desperate, which I hope means he'll make a mistake. I want this guy more every minute."

"I'll call Jo. I suspect she won't mind. We'll keep the curtains drawn so it looks like no one is there. I'll park in the barn. Let me know what you need."

"Hey, sorry I snapped at you. Text me when you get there."

"I will. Thanks."

"I'm going to get this maniac."

Tommy pulled his cruiser into a convenient doctor's parking space at the hospital. He got out and rushed through the main entrance, making his way to the floor and the alternate room JJ had been assigned.

Reece exited in time to almost collide. "Hey, you finally made it. I spoke with JJ about the USB drive. You wanna hear it from me or him?"

Tommy said nothing but held his hand out for the drive. Secured in his fist, he pushed into the room and heard Reece's footsteps on his heels.

He shook his head when Reece muttered, "That's what I thought."

Jo smiled, visibly brightened since Tommy had last seen her.

JJ grinned, appearing more like himself. The machines were disconnected, and his left hand squeezed a hard rubber ball, shifting it to the other without a thought. JJ asked, "Any good news, Chief Jager?"

Tommy almost laughed, then remembered Reece was behind him. He held up the USB between his thumb and forefinger. "What can you tell me about this?"

JJ evenly replied, "It's not mine. USB drives are like golf balls. Once you have a brand you prefer, you stick with it. I can't tell you what's on it without a computer to look at it."

Tommy considered his options. "If I plug it into my machine, it won't deliver a payload that captures my machine and flashes ransom demands, right?"

JJ shrugged. "I can't promise you that because I have no idea what it contains. I recommend you virus scan it on a low-value machine before you start inspecting the contents."

Tommy placed the device in his jeans pocket. "I'll look at it later in my office." He turned. "Reece, if the senator demands his drive, tell him I've got it for safekeeping. Don't tell him I will inspect it before returning it."

Reece shifted between his feet. "Are you good here so I can head home? It's getting late and—"

Tommy barked, "No. I need you here watching the senator and protecting Mr. Rodreguiz." He leveled a withering stare, then added, "Don't let anything happen to these folks or the senator. I'll be back later."

First Act

Vladimir circled the hospital at the twenty-mile-per-hour speed limit to assess the place when he saw the police cruiser depart. He parked between other vehicles toward the back of the lot, which allowed him to see the comings and goings.

"I'm ready to go," Mikhail announced with an anxious tone.

"Don't be in such a hurry. You must time your entrance with others to melt into the crowd and not draw attention. There will be security cameras, so keep your face lowered, just in case. When a group parks, you use them as a shield." Vladimir scanned the incoming cars. One parked not far from them, and several individuals emerged. "Ah, there is your cover. Go in with them. If they look at you, smile pleasantly and keep moving."

Mikhail grinned as he grabbed the handle. "You said his name is Rodreguiz, but you gave me no room number."

"Use your Lithuanian routine with broken English at a nurse's station," Vladimir replied. "You may have to visit several stations before finding the correct wing and the patient's location." Motioning with his hand, he added, "Go, get in with those visitors. I'll wait here for your return."

Mikhail scampered from the vehicle. Vladimir watched as he tagged along with the group and entered the building.

Mikhail noticed people lined up at a kiosk. When they typed in names, the room numbers appeared on the screen. He got in line and inched forward, trying not to be too impatient. He reached the front of the line and typed in the name. Nothing appeared except a note.

Please, Check Your Spelling

He tried four combinations and grinned when rewarded with a floor, wing, and room number. "How convenient," he said to the woman behind him, using his thick accent.

Mikhail went to the floor and wing, then slipped by the nurse's station and orderly staff. Opening the door, he discovered a freshly made bed, minus a patient. Confused, he left and returned to the nurse's station.

He looked at a nurse wearing pink scrubs with big eyes filling with water. He stammered in broken English. "Excuse me, Miss. Me came as a surprise to visit my childhood friend from Europe. I was told via family that he was in room two-one-two but was not there. Has he been repaired and sent home?"

The recently arrived duty nurse was charmed by the quaint request. She had noticed the room change when she checked on that patient an hour ago: "He was moved to two forty-one on the other side of the hall. His wife is with him, but he'd love the company. He's a great patient."

Delighted at the news, Mikhail moved stealthily and avoided eye contact to get to the correct room. As he approached, he noticed a tall, shapely brunette leaving. He admired her hip sway, as she left the area. He saw a man dozing in a chair and decided he was waiting for someone. When the sound of footsteps ended, he slipped into the room, grateful for the silent swing door.

Mikhail saw a form on the bed under covers in the dimly lit room. He moved too quickly and bumped into a chair. The form moved, and objects became apparent as the room was suddenly bathed in bright light.

Mikhail pulled his nunchaku from under his shirt and threateningly swung them in front of himself. He quietly demanded, "Are you the programmer who writes flawless viruses?"

JJ smirked. "How nice of you to visit." He held up the device next to his hand and pressed a button.

Mikhail ignored it as a threat. He closed the distance in a heartbeat. He renewed the demand, "I want the source code and the password to unlock our machines. If you cooperate, I'll be easy on you."

JJ picked up the food tray to his right and sent the glassware and dishes to the floor. He hurled the tray like a discus toward Mikhael in one smooth motion. The nunchaku blocked the tray in a blurred movement that sent it crashing to the floor.

Mikhail whirled his weapon to reinforce his demand, but the well-positioned pillow in JJ's hands stopped the stick.

"Making me mad will only earn you more hits. Give me the antidote. I'll let you live." Mikhail delivered two more blows in rapid succession, which were absorbed by the pillow just before impact.

"I wanted a rematch with you using my nunchaku," JJ complained, "not this stupid pillow."

Mikhail moved in to grab the pillow, stunned when he felt the dull knife and fork sink into his abdomen. He recoiled in pain and roared, "I'll get my information, and you'll die, Rodreguiz."

Mikhail prepared to lunge at JJ when the air shifted from the door opening. A split second later, a high-pitched hypersonic scream interrupted the combat. Mikhail turned to see the man from the hotel, the woman he'd seen leave, and a nurse inside the room. The man pointed his weapon. Mikhail targeted the man with his nunchaku in a last-ditch effort but missed. Next, he felt the impact as the man clubbed him with the butt of the gun and flung him against the wall. As he lay on the floor, he sensed the cuffs being tightened and smelled the stench of heavy breathing on his face. He closed his eyes, feeling defeated, when he heard, "Tommy, the fake Lithuanian, showed up in Rodreguiz's room. I've got him cuffed and sedated."

"Damn, I didn't miss him by much. Good work, Reece. His buddy is still on the loose. I'm on my way back. Tell the nurse and anyone else who wants to argue to get the Rodreguiz couple loaded into an ambulance. I want them moved within the hour. Jo will provide directions."

Before Mikhail slid into the darkness, he heard, "Did you bring two coffees, honey?"

CHAPTER 49

One Down, One to Go

"No, no, no," screamed Vladimir as the police cruiser parked at the hospital entrance. The pulsing blue and red lights caused him to slump lower in his seat. A tall man exited the car, scanned the parking lot, and hurried through the entrance.

The Russian slammed his hands on the steering wheel with so much force it wobbled. He sputtered, "Damn you, Mikhail. Something went wrong, or you would fly out a side door or shoot around from the back of the building. If you aren't running toward me, I hope you're dead so they can't make you talk." He punched his right fist into his other palm repeatedly. "I can't buy off these authorities like I could in Russia. You weren't supposed to fail," he lamented. "I give you five more minutes, my friend, and then I find that Lily person. She can't be gone from her business too long."

He watched the doors and noticed every departing visitor. "At least the two cars I'm between haven't moved, exposing my vehicle," he whispered, suddenly wanting a cigarette but unwilling to risk the smoke rising or the glowing tip.

Fifteen minutes passed before the tall officer emerged from the front door leading Mikhail. Vladimir saw his friend's arm being tightly gripped and handcuffs secured at his back. The prisoner shuffled like he was drugged, further infuriating Vladimir. "There's no way I'll be able to get him out again. Damn."

The officer opened the back door of his vehicle, roughly shoved Mikhail inside, and slammed the door. The man surveyed the parking lot again. The cop paused a heartbeat, glancing toward the SUV. "Don't look here," he prayed as he picked up his pistol beside him, ready to shoot first. "I bet they searched Mikhail and found no keys. This guy is smart. He thinks a ride is waiting."

He watched the officer slide into the driver's seat. A few moments later, the cruiser disappeared down the street.

Turning on his vehicle, he muttered, "Time to go." He slowly pulled out of the parking lot and left onto the highway opposite the cruiser's direction.

Tommy's impromptu parking lot inspection was interrupted by a call to his cell phone. "Reece, are JJ and Jo ready to leave yet?"

Reece grumbled, "I followed them down to the ER entrance to ensure they were safe. I watched them pull out. That's not what I'm calling about. The senator wigged out when I told him you took the USB drive for safekeeping. He has the whole hospital staff in an uproar. He's demanding this, that, and the thing in between, to the point he started throwing punches, and damned if he didn't knock my cigar to the floor."

Tommy laughed and then cleared his throat. "Reece, Senator David is suffering from post-traumatic shock because of the jailbreak which put him in the hospital. Explain the events to the doctor where he tried to hit you. Request the patient get sedated and physically restrained until he undergoes a psych evaluation. Do you agree?"

"Wow. Do you think the doctor would do that?"

"Pass on our recommendations," the chief insisted. "I'll talk to you later. I gotta take another call." He disconnected and answered his deputy. "Talk to me, Stuart."

"I'm in my car at Flower B&B, like you asked. A black SUV appeared a while ago and has circled twice so far. The vehicle paused, and the driver shined a light on the front door. Do you want me to intercept or follow?"

"Do not intercept!" Tommy said. "This guy is dangerous, and you don't have any backup nearby. You can follow at a distance. If he spots you, take evasive action. I think I know where he's headed. If he stops anywhere, text me the location. Thanks, Stuart."

"Yes, Chief."

CHAPTER 50

Circle the Wagons

Jo sat beside JJ in the ambulance, anxious to get home. The driver was oblivious to them because he was listening to his iPod.

JJ pouted. "They won't let me run the sirens or hit the lights on the trip. Poop."

Jo empathized as she stroked his jawline. "Honey, it'll be okay. There'll be other times when you get conked on the head, are in a coma for days, accused of murder, and gaily stalked by Russian mobsters wanting to kill you. We'll let you play in the ambulance then."

JJ laughed hysterically until Jo joined in the merriment. She pulled out her phone and placed a call. "Hi, Ann. There's been a plan change. We're headed home now instead of in the morning. We're in an ambulance with no lights, so don't be concerned. I'll operate the gate with my phone."

Ann advised, "Honey, we saw a truck there. It appeared a couple of hours ago. We thought it was you. Are we in trouble?"

Some panic gripped Jo until she recalled, "It's a big truck, right?"

"Yes."

"It must be Brandon and his tribe. Thanks for reminding me. He called earlier in the evening, and I forgot to let you know. It's all good."

"Sweetie, we're standing by if you need anything," Ann replied. "Lily's asleep in our guest room, resting after all the cleaning we did at your place and ours. Reminds me we need to get more whiskey."

"Thank you," said Jo. She looked at JJ and pressed another number. "Brandon, tell me you're at my house. JJ and I are on the way in the ambulance with no lights or sirens."

Brandon chuckled. "You almost forgot us? No worries, we've made ourselves at home. Boy, you're short on groceries. The house looks tidy, though."

"I'll have to tell you how community house cleaning is done in Texas sometime," she snorted. "Vladimir's sidekick attacked JJ at the hospital. Reece took him out. Tommy ordered us home. I believe this effort of herding us all into one location is called circling the wagons. I need to learn more about local cultural activities, I guess."

"I'm from New York. I've been informed to call anything I don't understand a Texas thang. The theory of circling the wagons is to have the wagons in a tight circle. Important souls, like children, are kept undercover in the center. Animals are in the center, too. Armed people scootch low and keep their backs to the center. The defenders hope no one can sneak up on the group from any direction as it is an armed circle. The technique dates back to John Ford's western movies, which he cranked out in the thirties and forties for Hollywood. It was patterned in films about pioneer migration west in the nineteenth century as a way to remain safe during Indian attacks."

Jo sighed. "There's so much to learn. We should be there in ten or fifteen, so please don't start circling the wagons until we're inside the gate."

"We'll be expecting you."

Tommy sat in his car outside his station. He drummed the fingers of one hand on the top of the steering wheel, glad the hospital suspect was secured, waiting for the feds to arrive. He decided to see if he could get some more pieces to fall into place.

"Herro," muttered the groggy reporter.

"Hey, Landon, it's Tommy. I know it's late, but I got something for you."

"Just a minute, Chief, let me grab my notepad and turn on the light."

"I don't have all night, Landon," said Tommy. "Based on the evidence discovered, we've jailed one of the men responsible for the murder of Adam Rawley. He refuses to talk, so we await the feds to supply his name. We believe his partner is an internationally wanted man, Vladimir Sokolov, who fled Russian authorities for criminal activities. Are you getting this, Landon?"

"Yep, I'm up now."

"Good. The motive for the murder appears to be blackmail. I'll send you a file with his photo and criminal record for filler."

"Wow, so Mr. Rawley was blackmailing people? Anyone else involved?"

"Not anything we want to see in the paper. I want Rawley's story and his photo on the front page of the morning paper, along with the suspect's picture, stating that a statewide manhunt is underway to arrest and detain the man. Any information citizens can provide to help lead to the arrest can be called into my office."

"This is great, Tommy. Can I add the information about Joyce at the scene yet?"

"Nope, not yet, but soon. No one else, either. You can say we have credible witnesses who have identified the men."

"All right, I'll use that. Thanks, Tommy."

"Hey, Landon, what have you ever heard about Senator David and his fundraising techniques?"

"Not much. I've been trying to find a chink in his armor for a while. No one seems to think he does anything for his district. I don't much care for his politics."

Tommy rubbed his jaw, thinking, then tapped his pocket to ensure the device was still there. "Me either, but he is our senator. I'll let you know when I have more."

"Thanks, man."

CHAPTER 51

The Reunion

It took Vladimir three slow passes around Flower B&B to be convinced Lily wasn't there. He paused and read the sign on the door indicating it was closed for water problems and decided it must be accurate.

"The time in Texas was supposed to be relaxing until I received that stupid letter," he ranted with a shake of his head. "Rawley had the nerve to try blackmailing me." He hit his chest with his fist. "Me, a master. Now he's dead, and I don't have the files he promised were on his laptop. My comrade from Mother Russia is locked up in a small-town jail." He swore loudly in his native language. When he reached the highway, he pointed his vehicle away from the café where the stupid girl worked. He took his eyes off the road and glanced up as he talked to himself. "Mikhail, you were clumsy and now in jail. We missed the best chance to get the computer geek at the hospital. If I stay any longer, they'll get me. I'd better…"

The piercing sound of an oncoming ambulance's horn interrupted his thoughts. He moved over to allow the vehicle to pass and avoid a collision.

"Get hold of yourself, Vlad," he counseled and took a breath. Watching the road, he continued his discussion with himself. "I don't need any traffic confrontation that might put me in front of the police." He screwed up his features and said, "That ambulance cut me off like it was an emergency, but there were no lights or sirens—just a horn. I need to check my map, but it's not heading toward the hospital, though I suppose there might be another around somewhere. Whether it's being dispatched or returning to the hospital, I'd expect a sense of urgency, which there was. Why no lights or sirens?"

Jo activated the application to release the gate. She supervised them when they arrived at the house as the ambulance techs helped JJ get out of the ambulance. They used a foldable wheelchair to bring him into the house. JJ stood at the threshold and stepped across.

Jo smiled at the techs. "Thank you for bringing us home safely. What was the horn honking about? Some animal in the road?"

"No," the tech said. "It was just someone in a big vehicle driving like my grandmother on her way home from church, slower than molasses pouring in December."

"Thanks again," she said, then closed and locked the door.

JJ shook hands with everyone and exchanged a few hugs. Jo guided him to a comfortable living room chair and insisted he sit, while she went to fix tea for them. Joyce joined to help.

JJ called, "Don't forget to close the front gate. The ambulance is gone."

"No, sweetheart, Tommy texted me he was on the way. He wants to speak to all of us about the next steps. I'm leaving the gate open for him."

Jason asked, "Jo, is it okay to watch a movie in the game room?"

"Sure, sweetie. I'd rather you do that than go outdoors. It's very late."

"Yes, ma'am."

Brandon sat next to JJ. Jo could overhear them discussing the latest pieces of the horrible drama.

"Joyce, how are you doing?"

"I'm nervous at times. It comes out of nowhere and grips me."

"I understand. You need to take care not to shut people out like I did."

"Tommy told Brandon about a doctor I might speak to at the college. I think I'll call as soon as this madman is caught."

Jo reached over and patted her arm. "Good idea. I'm here too if you ever need to talk." She put the finishing touches on the tea tray and added a few cookies saved from the party. "I think this is ready to go."

"I'll take the cookies and napkins and leave the hot beverage tray for you." Joyce held up her hands. "I get shaky, too."

As they turned the corner, Jo heard Brandon say, "Your Jo is quite the detective. She pulled together some remarkable clues and helped push to clear your name. She did it without revealing her remote support. I suspect that coworker of yours needs a pat on the back."

"I know, she's great. I'll pass along the thanks to our remote support."

She set down her tray in the center of the coffee table. Her phone rang when she started to pour. She retrieved her phone from her hip pocket and motioned they could each take it from there.

"Hi, Tommy. We made it home without incident, except the ambulance passed a slow grandma. I never saw it. We've got Brandon, Joyce, and Jason here. Lily is with Ann and Hank." She bent to pet the hound and added, "Max is here too."

Brandon motioned to get Jo's attention, "Ask him if it's okay for us to go shopping. The cupboards are bare, and we have a growing man to keep fed."

Jo giggled. "What about Jason?"

They all laughed.

"Tommy said you can go shopping as long as you get enough for him to have a Lily-style ham sandwich with pickles and chips. He's hungry, too."

Brandon looked at Max and said, "Let's get some food, buddy."

Max's tail thrummed like a kettle drum on the hard floor.

Joyce protested, "Better leave Max here. Food Guys grocery won't let you bring dogs unless they have service animal halters."

Brandon ruffled Max's ears. "Sorry, Max. You gotta stay here."

CHAPTER 52

Closing Time-One More Call

Vladimir made a right at the narrow road past the gate to the property and parked. "Yes!" He raised his arm in triumph. "I knew following the ambulance might work. The only thing that would make this better would be if that broad from the house arrived. I lucked into two birds with one stone. He kept an eye on the front door after the ambulance pulled away, having deposited a man in a wheelchair at the door.

"Mikhail," he said. "I have them exactly where I want them. I'll take care of this and then come free you. You'd appreciate this unbelievable stroke of luck, my friend."

He noticed several lights illuminate from inside and mused, "Your hit at the hospital must have spooked them. They've run home to hide." He rubbed his palms together and looked around to ensure his vehicle was concealed in dark shadows. "If I can get the protocol information I want from the geek, I'll pound this backwater hellhole with the virus. If I can't get you out, Mikhail, I'll trade you for the antidote to the virus."

Vladimir was about to leave and walk to the house because the gate was open when he observed a man exiting via the side door. The man headed toward the barn and disappeared inside. Seconds later, the barn doors opened. Vladimir laughed when he saw the big pickup emerge from the barn and head out of the gate back toward town.

Vladimir felt smug. "This is providence. That truck looked like the one at Joyce's place. Could I have both my problems together? How rich is that?"

He planned his attack. "I'll walk in, stick to the fence side, and avoid possible security cameras. I will have the advantage. When they discover me, it will be too late."

Jo paced around the living room.

JJ, trying to take a short nap, complained, "Honey, what is the matter? You keep moving and checking on things over and over. Frankly, you're wearing me out." He looked to Joyce for agreement, but she shrugged.

He felt her actions were uncharacteristic. She checked the camera feeds but came away just shaking her head. "I know, I'm sorry. I can't explain it. Something feels wrong."

JJ, a big believer in her intuition, cautiously asked, "Do I need to go on alert? I'm not at full capacity, but I can make a dent in someone's head if need be."

Jo checked the video camera one more time. She gasped and pointed. "There. There he is, moving between the shadows. I thought I saw something. He's here."

JJ nodded. "Babe, we've covered this scenario. I'll move to the other chair and pet Max. One light on me and turn off the rest. Joyce, please join Jason in the game room and lock the door."

Joyce rose and hastily complied.

JJ slowly made his way to the target chair. Max sat at his side, ready for attention. Jo switched off the lights and texted Tommy. Then she moved into the kitchen shadows. JJ heard her breathing routine as she inhaled and exhaled breaths, each to the count of ten. The side door clicked open. The dark intruder entered.

He seemed tall with broad shoulders. His steps were carefully placed to minimize sound.

JJ ruffled Max's ears, calming the low growl in the dog's throat. "Shush, Max. Mister, you've gotten this far. Come in, introduce yourself."

Vladimir boldly marched up to JJ, swinging his nunchaku in his right hand. He demanded, "I want the source code and passphrase to disarm it. Your virus has cost me a lot of time, and time doesn't come cheap."

"How did Rawley get your whereabouts?" JJ asked. "What was his leverage over you?"

"None of your concern."

"To a degree, he had some smarts." JJ sighed. "You're wanted on three continents by five governments, yet he pinned you down for some heavy crypto."

Swinging the nunchaku. Vladimir snarled, "This isn't a social call. You're not a podcast show host. Just give me the virus code and the passphrase to unlock that jerk's laptop. He promised me his blackmail list as compensation for my trouble."

JJ snorted. "Rawley did the same thing to you that I did to him. He followed all the spam you sent out with ransomware viruses backward through the anonymizing servers and threatened you directly. I'll bet that was a shocker to you and your buddy. Getting blackmailed wasn't what you expected, was it?"

Vladimir growled and closed the distance, the weapon making a harsh whirling sound as he spun it. JJ spotted a thunderous expression. "Never laugh at Vladimir! You're going to…"

JJ noticed Jo as she came behind the intruder like a cat on its silent paws. She let loose a wail of the Valkyries, and, with all her strength, delivered a mighty blow to Vladimir's head with her cast iron skillet—the resounding klong convinced JJ of the power of the impact.

Vladimir crumpled to the floor. Jo stood over him, breathing hard, and delivered two crushing blows to each of his hands in succession. JJ winced at the sound of bones crunching.

He realized she was working on adrenaline and was about to bash Vladimir in his head again.

"Jo, honey, how about that tea? I'm thirsty. He's out for the count."

Jo inhaled and closed her eyes. She trembled as she placed the frying pan on the coffee table and plopped into the closest chair.

A few minutes later, she declared, "You don't get to hurt my husband ever again."

CHAPTER 53

Frying Pan Queen
Reigns Supreme

Jo watched while JJ secured Vladimir's hands behind his back. She held the skillet, bouncing up and down on her bare toes, waiting for another reason to use it again.

JJ looked at her and grinned. "Tommy's cruiser just pulled in. I think he is going to like your present, Jo."

Tommy entered through the side door and did a double-take when he saw Jo with her pan. He shifted his gaze to JJ, who was getting off the floor with Vladimir lying face-down.

Tommy looked around. "Where is everybody?"

Jo relaxed, walked with the skillet inside the kitchen, and hung it on the rack above the stove. "We spotted him in the camera feed sneaking in, moving between shadows after Brandon left to shop. Joyce is in the game room with Jason. JJ played the bait role perfectly. Vladimir swallowed it, and I took him out. My gift to you, Tommy."

JJ muttered, "I need to tune those cameras so I don't miss the next intruder."

Tommy chuckled, "Let me guess, frying pans-R-Us? When I give him to the feds, do I say he needs medical treatment?"

"I don't care if his hands ever work again, so it's your choice."

Silence reigned for a few moments.

"Can we get Joyce out here to confirm or deny this is the assassin she saw at Rawley's?" Tommy asked. "Do you think she is strong enough to do that? Brandon wasn't sure."

"Let me ask her," said Jo. "This might give her closure on what she witnessed."

Jo went to the game room and returned with Joyce and Jason.

Tommy looked at JJ. "She's a tough noodle, JJ. She's been there every step of the way to help find this murderer. She even got into my face once about you being a suspect."

"I'm not giving her up if that is what you're hoping for. However, it would be best if you took full credit for the take-down. We're trying to enjoy the simple country life and don't want any publicity here at our vacation home."

Jo beamed, realizing they weren't moving. Joyce was almost glued to her side, looking at Tommy. Jo prodded, "You can do this. Face your fears, Joyce. You're heading for closure."

Tommy stepped in front of Vladimir. "Joyce, are you up for this? He's out cold. He can't hurt you or anyone. Yours is the last puzzle piece, but if you won't, we'll…"

Joyce set her jaw and looked straight at Tommy. "After all my friends have done for me, the least I can do is to try. Tommy, let me see him. I'll tell you the truth."

Jo patted her back. The chief stepped to one side and rolled Vladimir over to show his face. Joyce choked back a cry, covered her eyes with her hands, and groaned. For a moment, Jo rubbed a circle on her back.

Joyce lowered her hands to her sides, focused on the tied-up prisoner. "May I have another light and stand in front of him Tommy? I want to be sure."

Tommy nodded, and Jo flipped a switch to brighten the space. Joyce circled the unconscious man. "That's him, Tommy. It's too bad I can't see his eyes. They appeared vicious in the reflection of the mirror in the hallway."

Tommy bent and added handcuffs to Vladimir as Brandon returned. Opening the door, he hollered, "Can I get assistance carrying everything in? I cleaned out the store."

"Brandon, we need your help carrying something out first," Joyce hollered.

Brandon stepped into the area, smirking. "Is this mister-black SUV who's been stalking everyone?"

"He dropped by to deliver a beating and get the antidote to JJ's computer virus. Instead, *he* got clonked and a nice shiny pair of handcuffs."

"Tommy, I can call Lily and get her to verify his identity. She's at Ann's."

"He's the man Lily had dinner with," Brandon said, "His face matches the photo I took, Tommy."

"Agreed. Brandon. Help me heft this unwanted trash into my cruiser. I can put him in a nice cell next to his buddy. I expect the feds here in the morning." Tommy turned to JJ. "Can you tell me what's on this drive?" He held up the device Reece secured from the senator.

"Sure. Will tomorrow morning work? I'm tired."

"Of course, no problem."

"Chief, we haven't gotten the rental, so I'm without transportation. Can I get a ride to pick it up from the impound yard?"

Brandon interjected, "If Vladimir drove his SUV here, you'll need someone to drive it back to the station. From there, it's just a quick hop over to the impound yard."

"I hate to ask you to do that. Instead…" Tommy called his deputy. "Stuart, I need a favor. Please retrieve Rodreguiz's vehicle using the duplicate key I had made and deliver it to their house. Once you're there, drive the suspect's vehicle back to the impound yard. I'll text you the license plate."

Jo delivered her best model smile. "Thank you. That was very kind." She grinned, "Nice of you to think of an extra key, too."

Jason walked in with three grocery sacks. "How about we get food in? I'm starved."

"Yes, of course," Jo agreed. "Tommy's ham sandwich is first, so he can enjoy it while taking this trash to the cell in town."

JJ moved back over to be seated comfortably next to his PC. He noticed a live feed of Brayson. "Thanks for all that remote support," he said softly. "We trapped the adversary, and nobody but the blackmailer was killed. Some of us have a few bruises."

Brayson chuckled. "Stay in relaxing Magnolia Bluff for a while. Heal up? If I need you, you can work from there. But before I disconnect, what is the passphrase to disable that nifty computer virus? I might have need of it sometime."

JJ chuckled. "You want the passphrase that will unlock the computer and disinfect it? Is that what I'm hearing? Because it's you, the passphrase is…ready? J-O-W."

Brayson glared through the screen and moaned, "Three letters, that's it? Are you serious?"

JJ retorted, "I was in a hurry."

CHAPTER 54

Friends of Fiends

Jo smoothed JJ's hair from his face in the morning light as he slept. She lovingly studied his robust features while she sipped coffee.

JJ's eyes fluttered open. He grinned. "I was dreaming about our Brazilian dark roast coffee." He glanced at the cup. "Do you have any more?"

Jo looked at JJ with that deep, penetrating stare, her Expresso brown eyes inviting amorous responses. They simultaneously sighed when Tommy's cruiser rolled up to a stop near the house.

"We need to change the gate code, so he's forced to make a request."

The corners of her lips lifted. "Good idea. I'll make you coffee. Come out when you're ready."

Turning back in the doorway, she mischievously remarked, "Count on us revisiting this moment tonight, Mr. Rodreguiz."

JJ smiled.

She could read his mind.

Jo and the chief had completed the niceties when JJ entered the kitchen area. Jo frowned, seeing him move slower than normal. She laid out a cup for him.

"Thank you, sweetheart." JJ took a huge sip. "Ambrosia. I assume Tommy got the regular rather than the high-octane."

They all chuckled.

"Let's look at the thumb drive. Maybe we can unlock Rawley's laptop, Chief," said JJ.

JJ led the way to his study. He sat at his workstation computer. He powered it up, adding his password credentials. Tommy handed Rawley's laptop to JJ. He turned it on, while he connected a cord so Tommy could watch the results on the big screen. The virus message appeared. Jo flinched. JJ's fingers flew on the keyboard. Another screen demanded a passphrase. Three keystrokes later, the machine's content appeared. Tommy shook his head with the same amazement as Jo. She would ask him later which three letters he entered.

"The passphrase sanitizes the virus, restores access to all the files, and erases the virus program," JJ stated. "You can review all the files." He unkinked his back with a twist in the chair. "Next, let's see what the USB drive contains."

The drive opened, and JJ rapidly scanned through the data. Then he opened the files on Rawley's machine. "Brother, Rawley was a real noodle. He had some talent, but his machine was an open book. Nothing is password protected and camouflaged from its original intent." JJ split the information between the two big display screens to compare the laptop to the thumb drive and shook his head. "Look, here is a subdirectory for Senator David on Rawley's PC. These files," he circled a group, "match what's on the USB drive."

Jo spotted the similarities. She saw Tommy recognized the items, as he slapped his hand against his head.

After several minutes of opening and scanning files on the thumb drive, JJ said, "Each of these donor document files has notes regarding leveraging information gathered. Not quite blackmail conviction content, but he wasn't compiling this background information on these people to send them birthday or Christmas cards."

"Is it possible the good senator hired Rawley to create a list of donors with squishy backgrounds he could use to influence campaign contributions?" the chief mused. "No wonder we couldn't figure out how he consistently got re-elected."

"Here's the directory for Vladimir and all the dirt on him," JJ added. "Ugh, this is repugnant material. Look at everything Rawley assembled to denounce the man as a Russian gangster. Stupid to try to blackmail him, though."

"JJ," Tommy asked, "I know it's a lot to ask, but can you break into Rawley's email account?"

"That's not a very ethical approach to detective work. Hacking into someone's email account without court authority is a problem. However, if we used this file he called PASSWORDS, it wouldn't be hacking but respectfully reviewing a deceased person's personal effects to alert the next of kin." JJ quickly opened the email account. Jo watched the chief's eyes reading the information as it filled the screen.

"JJ, I want you to know I'm sorry I couldn't use you to retrieve the data. You were recovering from your injuries, so I had the feds help me extract this data from Rawley's machine. I'll ensure you and Jo are minimized in my reports. I won't share anything with the newspaper about your involvement. I have all the evidence I need for the feds to prosecute the two Russians for the murder of Rawley and Vladimir for the brutal beating of Stacie, a waitress at the big truck stop located two miles down the interstate."

Jo grinned at JJ. "Thank you, Chief."

The conversation was interrupted by a text and a call to Tommy's cell phone.

The chief glanced at the text and answered his phone. "Don't tell me you have another problem, Reece."

"Chief, I have a lady who came in to enter a formal complaint against Senator David."

Tommy tilted his head, confused. "A formal complaint? What?"

"You're not going to believe this, Chief, but it's the rising country singer Abby Rose. She saw a flyer for a rally featuring Senator David when she stopped for supper before her tour bus left Texas. She's claiming he, along with some photographer, staged a shot where David ripped her custom-designed, purple sequined bodice when he was, um, groping her with one of his hands. She spotted a morning edition of our newspaper online and insisted the photographer was Adam Rawley."

Tommy laughed for a minute straight before he regained control. "Take her statement, Reece, and thank her for coming forward." He disconnected. "Oh, brother. This takes the cake. Senator David worked with Rawley for a while, building his reelection treasure chest."

He chuckled and called Landon. "Hey, got an additional story for you."

He relayed the details and disconnected.

"This is picture perfect." He chuckled again. "The blackmailer is dead, the cyberthugs will be behind bars indefinitely, and Senator David will retire by morning." He rubbed his hands together with a Cheshire cat expression.

"Tommy," Jo asked, "will the newspaper reporter discuss our involvement?"

"Already done. Landon swore he wouldn't do anything to bring attention to the Cast Iron Queen. He also said the entire town would protect you because both of you are a part of the community. You and JJ are wonderful neighbors."

Tommy smiled wistfully. "One last detail and I'm taking a break for a day or two." He pressed a number from the contact list on his phone. It connected. "Lily. Are you ready to leave? You need to serve breakfast tomorrow morning…Great, I'll be there in ten minutes."

Tommy snapped his phone to the hip-holder. "I promised I'd take her home for one of her ham sandwiches. Sorry, Jo, hers are the best."

Book Club Member Questions for

The Ransom Enigma

Breakfield and Burkey are happy to spend time with your book club in person or via a virtual meeting. Reach out to them at *Authors@EnigmaSeries.com*. Special discounts apply to book clubs with ten or more members on any of their stories. Please *post a review on Goodreads, Amazon, BookBub, and Barnes and* Noble. Thank you.

Did you like how Jo was portrayed in *The Ransom Enigma*?

Would you have enjoyed attending the party at her new home in Magnolia Bluff?

What would Jo have done if JJ had died, and how would you have wanted to comfort her?

Which story revelation surprised you the most?

Who was the most despicable character, and why?

Did you like how Brandon stepped up to help Jo?

Was his previous experience as a detective a positive addition to the evolution of the story plot?

Have you ever been as terrified as Joyce was? Did you find her response believable?

Who was your favorite character in this story?

If you ever go to Magnolia Bluff, which of the places you know of from the series would you want to visit?

Would you like to see Jo and JJ return in a future installment?

Do you think Joyce and Brandon have a future?

How many Magnolia Bluff Crime Chronicles stories have you read and reviewed?

Does *The Ransom Enigma* make you want to read them all?

For Boys Who Struggle with Darkness
By Richard Schwindt
The Magnolia Bluff Crime Chronicles: Book 28

Friday night

Sheriff Buck Blanton seemed in a mood for reminiscence. In uniform, he leaned back against the east wall of O'Garas bar and began to talk about Billy Hamilton. A big man, Buck grinned as he spoke. He always grinned as he spoke.

"You know Mike, I first had to talk to Billy when he was just a teenager." Buck's eyes seemed to defocus, as if lost in history. "He'd attempted to force some moves on young Sue Hope, now Sue Kurelek, and she responded with some moves her father had taught her. Her daddy learned those tricks in the Marine Corps."

Buck chuckled through his grin. "Billy still had an ice pack over his nuts when he called the police to complain she had assaulted him. All I could do was laugh, and tell him that next time he tried a stunt like that, I would make sure that a simple ice pack would not begin to suffice."

The sheriff maintained an old school approach when it came to keeping riff-raff and malcontents in line. I was sure that threat meant exactly what it implied.

Now he sighed. "I have had to have a little talk with him twice since then concerning ill treatment of his wife. Now it looks like we need another chat."

Billy, a foot to one side of Buck, stiffened and gurgled. He would have said something but for my hand, wrapped around his throat, pinning him to the wall, forcing him up onto tiptoes. He understood what a "chat" with Sheriff Buck entailed.

Blanton wasn't finished. "Mike, I don't have to be Sherlock Holmes to know the origins of your anger."

I chuckled, despite my rage, at the comparison. Hard to imagine two individuals more unalike than Buck Blanton and Sherlock Holmes. Maintaining my grip on Billy, I tossed the shot of bourbon in my glass and slammed it down on the table behind me.

Rita Hamilton had appeared in my office this morning, stiff from last night's beating, shamed by the ragged grape-colored bruise that descended from her right eye to the corner of her mouth.

Even after spending the session coaxing Rita from behind the terror that infused her, I might have been okay if…

"Hey Hans." Buck called over to deputy sergeant Hans Winkler, now occupying his usual stool at the bar. "Billy been bragging about keeping his wife in her place again?"

Hans had been studiously ignoring my encounter with Billy, even while distracting the bartender's notice. I had no idea who called Buck.

He responded: "Yes, indeed he has, Buck. How it's no one's business but his own. I was going to put on some work clothes tomorrow, and go and check in on Mrs. Hamilton. In the meantime, I would have intervened if Mike's bit of fun had gotten out of hand."

Buck turned his attention back to me. Though an older man, he was big and strong. I had it on good authority that in the wrong company he could be mean as a snake. No one in their right mind fucked with him.

Billy followed the conversation, bloodshot eyes moving from side to side.

Buck was back now, staring ahead. "Mike, I may not be Sigmund Freud, but I suspect some displacement activity here."

Sigmund Freud? What went on in Buck Blanton's head?

But between my intoxication and rage, I began to dimly see that my unconscious mind was driving the bus.

"You have had a bad week, Mike. Real bad. And I don't want to see it get worse. I want to see Billy Hamilton's week get worse, but not my friend, Dr. Mike Kurelek. You see, we all have our station in the world. You are a doctor and healer. I keep the peace. The natural order of things is that I take custody of Mr. Hamilton, we go for our chat, and you step out into the hot Texas night, head home, and spend the rest of the evening with your pretty wife."

He had a point.

I lowered Billy to the floor, looked into his eyes and said gently. "You fuck with me or your wife again, and I will tear your liver out."

Buck grinned. "Nicely said, Mike. Now give me your truck keys."

I reached into my pocket and handed them over. "You want me to walk it off?"

"Just walk out the door."

With one last glare at Billy, I headed into the sweltering late August evening. I stood for a moment, taking in the slash of humidity, before I noticed a car idling towards one side of the lot. I ambled over and entered through the passenger side.

"How drunk are you, Mike?"

"So-so, Sue. You?"

"Very funny. I have two months left before your daughter arrives, then you're doing the damn driving around Magnolia Bluff."

"I'm sorry darling. I shouldn't have left you alone tonight."

"Mike, I'm the one who told you to get out and blow off some steam with Winkler, and whoever else was hanging out at O'Garas."

"You're traumatized and seven months pregnant. I shouldn't have left."

Sue glanced down at the large belly that awkwardly held up the seatbelt. Cold waves of air conditioning blew into the car. "Wednesday was hard on both of us. I care about Jack as much as you, and we are going to the medical center tomorrow together to see him."

A tear ran down my cheek. I didn't want to cry in front of my wife.

She tried to cheer me up: "What did you do to Billy Hamilton?"

"He'll be mostly whispering, and on a soft diet for a few days, but I think Buck might do the real damage."

Sue snorted, and replied in her deep Texas drawl. "Mike, you're the amateur here. Buck will scare the living shit out of him, but he won't leave marks."

I began to see some light through my intoxication. "Sue, how do you know about Billy Hamilton?"

Then, "Did you call Buck Blanton?"

"Of course, I did, dumbass. Rita Hamilton called me after you left the house. She was scared. She'd hurt Billy's feelings by going to a therapist. You were trying to break up her marriage. Billy had a call from a buddy at O'Garas. He was going to confront you."

Sue put her car into gear. "Let's head home. We can get your truck in the morning. I don't want to leave Butch alone too long."

"Were you scared Billy would hurt me?"

Now she laughed out loud, putting a hand on her distended belly. It looked like it hurt.

"I sure hope the new Kurelek is smarter than the old one. Billy hurt you? That pathetic little weasel is one of nature's great cowards. Why do you think he beats on women?"

Her tone changed: "With… what happened… I honestly thought you might kill him. Mike, you're a psychologist with the body of a middle linebacker, and the ability to kill. That ever gets set loose… I don't want to lose you."

"With… what happened…" I looked over at my wife. "We can't even talk about it. What are we going to do?"

"You are going to do what you do best. Your friend needs help now. I need to stay strong."

"You shouldn't have to, Sue."

"Don't patronize me, Mike. We stay strong together."

"I love you."

"I love you too."

WEDNESDAY NIGHT, TWO DAYS EARLIER

For a born and bred Texas girl, Sue had some strange friends. We were laughing together as we danced in our living room, following dinner with Alicia and Kyle, who had recently exited California for the Lone Star State.

I had managed through the conversation, and somehow ingested the vegan dinner. Just amazing what you can do with an artichoke. The organic wine, on the other hand, was delicious, and Kyle had twice returned to his wine rack to keep my glass full.

Sue was in high spirits, despite the heat. The air conditioning unit in our house had been unreliable of late as the temperature hovered near 100 degrees during the day. I assumed the third trimester would take the shine off that energy, but it hadn't happened yet. In a few moments I anticipated we would start drifting towards the bedroom.

We both turned as a strange sound came from our door, a mix between a scratch and a moan.

"What's that, Mike?"

"You heard it too?"

I released her warm body, reoriented towards the front door, and opened it.

Sue turned white, tottered on her feet and sat down. Every muscle in my body stiffened.

Butch, my neighbor Jack Rice's coon hound, limped through the door on three paws. He was bleeding from his nose, and both ears. He whimpered in pain. He'd come to us.

We stared in silence for only a moment. Sue was headed towards Butch, but I stopped her.

"I want you to call the police, but first, go to the bedroom and get me your Glock." She turned and disappeared, reappearing moments later with the gun and a full mag.

I shoved in the mag, racked a round into the chamber, and flicked the safety. Then I ran out the door.

Jack's door was open. I called in: "Hey Jack, it's Mike. You okay?"

Silence. I carefully stepped in, sidearm at the ready.

I found him almost right away. He was laying very still, face smashed, bleeding, like Butch, from nose and ears. One prosthetic leg lay at a ninety-degree angle. The other had been ripped from the stump, and tossed to the side.

Sucking in my breath, I realized that I needed to search his small house first. If whoever had done this was still here…

That didn't take long, it was a small bungalow, and I returned to his side. Who the hell would do this to a seventy-five-year-old veteran?

UNDERGROUND AUTHORS AND THE MAGNOLIA BLUFF CRIME CHRONICLES

AN AUTHORS CO-OP

The late Caleb Pirtle III organized the Underground Authors in mid-2020. The purpose was to harness the collective reach of a dozen authors to promote each other's books.

Writers like to write. It didn't take long for the group to come up with the idea to create a member collection of short stories with a central theme to aid the joint marketing efforts.

Beyond the Sea: Stories from the Underground was published in April 2021. (Pick up a copy from Amazon) The group adopted their name—Underground Authors.

Little did the authors realize that *Beyond the Sea's* publication would change things in unexpected ways.

MAGNOLIA BLUFF

In May 2021, following an online writers conference, CW Hawes proposed that the Underground Authors write a multi-author series. After a flurry of emails, the group sketched out the broad picture of the town, the important landmarks, and the main characters writers would use in his or her books. Magnolia Bluff Crime Chronicles was born.

The series revolves around the goings-on in the small, fictional Texas Hill Country town of Magnolia Bluff. Each author chronicles our small town's lives, loves, and deaths. There are a dozen different perspectives on life in Magnolia Bluff, Texas—a beautiful little place on the shore of Burnet Reservoir, where murder waits in the wings.

We are in our third season, and Magnolia Bluff has taken on a life of its own. The town has become a real place for the writers and readers, and the characters are real people.

We are delighted at the fabulous reception the series has received. It's exciting to know we created something readers find a bit unique in the world of crime fiction.

We hope you enjoyed this story and invite you to consider the other episodes in the ongoing Magnolia Bluff saga. If this is your first visit, you are in for a delightful treat. And if you are a returning reader visitor, you know you will find humor, suspense, and people you care about.

All the best, and be sure to look behind you both ways before entering the crosswalk.

—The Underground Authors

Breakfield–Charles is a data/telecom solution architect and supports digital security, block-chain solutions, and unified communications. He enjoys writing, studying World War II history, travel, and cultural exchanges. Charles' love of wine, cooking, and Harley riding often provides writing topics. Much of his personality comes from his father, who served in the military for 30 years and three wars. Charles grew up on multiple bases and in different countries. The multicultural exposure helps him with the various character perspectives they bring to the series. His ambition is to continue to teach Burkey humor.

Burkey–Rox is a Customer Experience Specialist who works with businesses worldwide. As a gifted speaker and accomplished listener, she bridges the chasm between business problems and technical solutions to optimize business productivity. She has written technology documents and white papers but launched into high gear when plotting their next techno-thriller or short story. She led the other kids with her highly charged imagination as a child, generating new adventures with make-believe characters. She is proud of being a Girl Scout until high school and con-tributed to the community as a member of a Head Start program. Rox enjoys her family, learning, listening to people, traveling, outdoor activities, sewing, cooking, and thinking about diversifying the series.

Breakfield and Burkey began their partnership writing non-fiction papers and books. They formed a business partnership to write as fictional storytellers. They recognize this oral tradition as an evolving method to deliver excitement, thrills, and insights into today's technology risks. They are passionate about leveraging accurate technology into fictional writing. The variety of characters in their series has attributes of the many people who crossed their professional paths. Admittedly, Breakfield often asks exciting people he meets if they thought about being an evil cyberthug or femme fatale in their series.

Both authors have traveled to many places around the world. These travels are pulled into stories that require actual knowledge of specific locals. They enjoy well-rounded thrillers, including humor, romance, intrigue, suspense, and mystery. They love to talk about their stories at private book readings or events both public and private. You can learn where they will be from the calendar on their website: *https://www.EnigmaSeries.com/*

Their website is routinely updated with new interviews, answers to readers' questions, book trailers, and contests. You may also find it fascinating to check out the fun acronyms they create for the stories summarized on their website. Reach out to them at *Authors@EnigmaSeries.com, Twitter @EnigmaSeries,* or *Facebook @TheEnigmaSeries.*

We invite you to provide a fair and honest review on Amazon and any other places you post reviews.

Thank you for your feedback.

MAGNOLIA BLUFF CRIME CHRONICLES SEASON 1

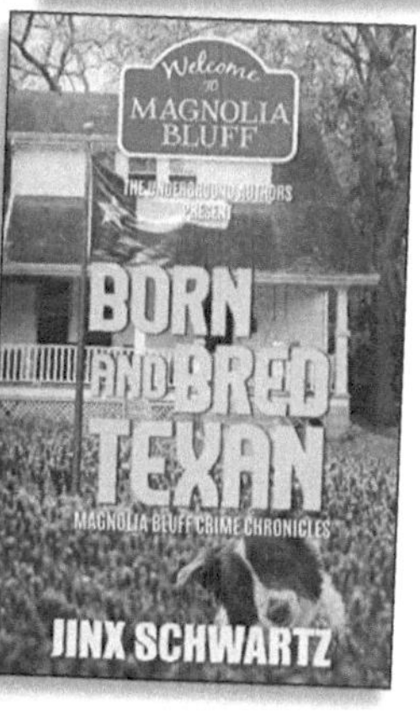

MAGNOLIA BLUFF CRIME CHRONICLES: SEASON 2

MAGNOLIA BLUFF CRIME CHRONICLES: SEASON 3

We would greatly appreciate
if you would take a few minutes
and provide a review of this work
on Amazon, Goodreads
and any of your other favorite places.

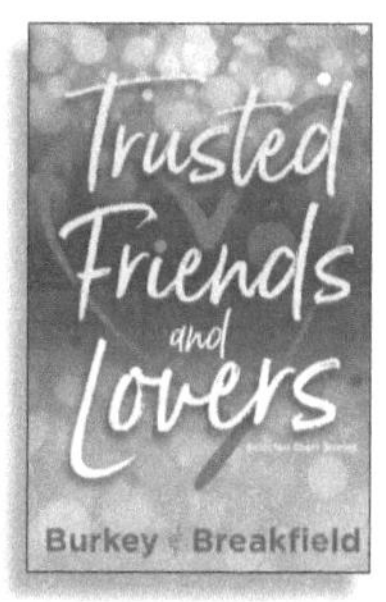

Other stories by Breakfield and Burkey in
the Heirs Series are at **www.EnigmaBookSeries.com**